ABBOTT AWAITS

YELLOW SHOE FICTION
Michael Griffith, Series Editor

A NOVEL

ABBOTT AWAITS

CHRIS BACHELDER

Louisiana State University Press)|(Baton Rouge

Published by Louisiana State University Press
Copyright © 2011 by Chris Bachelder
All rights reserved
Manufactured in the United States of America
LSU Press Paperback Original

Designer: Mandy McDonald Scallan
Typeface: text, Whitman; display, Helvetica Neue

Library of Congress Cataloging-in-Publication Data

Bachelder, Chris.
  Abbott awaits : a novel / Chris Bachelder.
    p. cm. - (Yellow shoe fiction)
  ISBN 978-0-8071-3722-2 (pbk. : alk. paper)
  I. Title.
  PS3602.A34A65 2011
  813'.6 - dc22

                                        2010024227

The paper in this book meets the guidelines for permanence
and durability of the Committee on Production Guidelines for
Book Longevity of the Council on Library Resources. ∞

for the wonders—
Jennifer, Alice, Claire

O the evening robin, at the end of a New England summer day! If I could ever find the twig he sits upon!

—Thoreau, *Walden*

CONTENTS

ABBOTT AWAITS

The bulb in the desk lamp burned out eleven days ago, yet Abbott
continues to twist the knob every time he sits down. It's habit, not hope,
Abbott thinks, though he pauses over the distinction. He sits in the dark,
awaiting connection. Across the hallway there is no light beneath Abbott's
bedroom door, which means his wife is either asleep or not asleep. She
is an insomniac, and six months pregnant. Would he wake her if New
York were rubble and ash? Charlotte? But tonight the empire is more
or less intact. Abbott clicks "Child tied in hot car as couple dines," but
he discovers that the article fails to answer the questions raised by the
headline. For instance, Why do people do things? And just what is going
on? Given the restaurant in whose parking lot the child, 9, was allegedly
tied, the verb *dines* seems to Abbott not only inaccurate but editorially
wicked. Elsewhere, a former celebrity has chosen death over middle age.
A sleeping-bag prank has taken a life. A trap door has revealed a dungeon.
In smaller type, the functioning and malfunctioning of military equipment has killed many, many people, all of whom, Abbott presumes, would
rather have continued to exist, in spite of everything. Abbott's yard needs

mowing, he remembers. He ought to go to bed. He knows that sleep is necessary for temperament, energy, long- and short-term memory, healthy skin, brain, heart, back, and feet. There are people who *die* of sleeplessness. But tonight at a righteous, low-traffic site he finds a photo essay about a Chernobyl orphanage, two decades after the Mishap. There is a warning about disturbing images. He cannot very well turn away now, lest he be someone who turns away from the disturbing. But first, Abbott's six-point safety check: (1) *time* (12:42 A.M.); (2) *child monitor* (quiet); (3) *light beneath bedroom door* (no light); (4) *strength of dial-up Internet connection* (49.6 Kbps); (5) *tall stack of final exams* (half-graded); (6) *fluid level of cocktail glass* (low). Abbott walks through the dark house to the kitchen to top off his drink, then returns to the dark office. It's not as if there aren't packages of light bulbs in the hall closet. He settles into his chair, turns the knob of the lamp. He knows this one is going to hurt: slow-loading photographs of deformed and radioactive children, while his own developmentally normal child sleeps down the hall in her blue-and-green pajamas. Her skin is perfect. He minimizes the running box score of the West Coast ball game, and then, already disturbed, selects a disturbing image.

June

1 Abbott Visits the Pet Store

One should always be wary of a pet store that is also a soft-drink outlet, but it's a sunny morning in the Pioneer Valley of Western Massachusetts and Abbott is prepared to embrace the world. Moreover, he needs to kill another hour while his wife gets some sleep in the quiet house. On the drive from the coffee shop, he finds his sunglasses in a pouch on the passenger door, and he puts them on for the first time this season. The glasses feel strange on his nose and ears. They're nearly ten years old. Perhaps this will be the summer he is finally able to break or lose them. "Ready?" he says to his two-year-old daughter, pulling her out of the car seat. In the parking lot the girl points up and says, "Moon!" Abbott looks up skeptically, but sure enough. Grown people walk past carrying small bags of fish or crickets. They smile at the man with the premillennial shades and the curly-headed girl. Once inside the pet store/soft-drink outlet, Abbott regrets the outing immediately. The smell, for one thing. And all that sad rustling and chirping. His daughter begins to squirm, and when he places her on the ground, she scuttles to a tall rotating rack of plastic birds whose function, Abbott is dismayed to learn, is to keep real

pet birds from getting lonesome. They are called Amigos. The girl pulls a
low one from the rack and runs to the guinea pigs, who are either sleeping or deceased. She zigzags down the tragic aisle, from the hidden ham-
sters to the nibbling rabbits to the lizards basking beneath yellow bulbs.
Many of the animals, warm-blooded and cold-, have their faces pushed
into back corners of cages or aquariums. At a point far down the aisle,
Abbott notices, the enclosures begin to contain animals that are retail
food for other animals: the flies, worms, grubs, cockroaches, ants, and
crickets. "There," the girl says. "That." She presents her Amigo to a bored
scorpion. The end of the aisle, at which stands a life-sized cardboard cutout of someone Abbott does not recognize, turns out not to be the end of
the aisle. The passage continues dimly beneath a burned-out fluorescent
tube. Abbott's daughter runs past the life-sized cutout, losing a shoe and
not caring. Abbott retrieves the shoe and follows. He has that feeling
that the inside of this building is larger than the outside. At the very end
of the aisle, across from stacked cases of root beer and cream soda, he
sees a glass tank full of brightly colored party favors. His daughter sees it
too, and hobbles there with a floppy sock. Approaching the tank in the
low light, he observes that it is filled with plastic snails in garish colors.
Coming closer still, following his daughter, he realizes that the aquarium
contains hermit crabs—real ones—whose shells have been painted,
whereupon Abbott suffers an elaborate reaction. He cannot help wondering, first of all, who paints these crabs. It is not difficult to imagine the
makeshift assembly lines, the improper ventilation, the fingers marred by
repetitive motion and claw cuts. He speculates that crab painting does not
fulfill what he considers the fundamental human need to create beauty.
Immobilized on the sticky floor, he is also curious about the relative
evolutionary histories of the two species here associated. Fossils of hermit
crabs, he will later learn on the Internet, have been traced to the Late
Cretaceous period, meaning that these creatures originated 65 to 100 million years ago. Meanwhile, *Homo sapiens* (*sapiens* meaning intelligent or
wise) emerged approximately two hundred thousand years ago, at which
point they immediately, relatively speaking, began decorating other species. Abbott watches the purple crab with the yellow swoop approach the
pink crab with the blue zigzag, and while he is not sure if hermit crabs

have a central nervous system, he hopes that if they do, it is insufficiently complex to generate feelings of shame or humiliation. He is, he thinks, opposed to animal painting across the board, but at this moment he feels that the hermit crab is a particularly inappropriate knickknack. This is not, let's face it, a festive creature, and the pastel whorls are, rather than fun or cute, unseemly and dispiriting. Naturally there is, for the serious fan, a Red Sox crab, blue with a red B, alone in a corner of the tank. Abbott bends to study it, and when he sees that it is scavenging chips of lime green craft paint, he feels the electric snap in his chest that can only mean his heart has tripped its circuit again. "Pretty," Abbott's daughter says, her palms and nose pressed against the smudged glass. "Have one?" she asks. All the parenting experts, whose advice Abbott's wife passes on to Abbott in radically abridged form, suggest that you use the word *No* as infrequently as possible when speaking to your toddler. "No," Abbott says. He picks her up, sets her off. "Let's go," he says. "Time for home."

2 Abbott and the Somersault

On the stained carpet in the family room, Abbott gently flips his daughter over on her head in a near approximation of a somersault. "Somersault," he says. "Dad do it?" she says. "OK," he says. He is, after all, on his summer break. He clears away the books and animals to make room. This is fun physical play with his child; the body is a wondrous instrument. "OK, watch this," he says, sensing her attention already shifting to a stuffed chipmunk. He prepares but then stops to wonder if what he's envisioning is actually a somersault. He hasn't thought about somersaults in years, maybe decades. What he is doing—or what he is preparing to do—does not seem like a somersault. It can't be a somersault. For one thing, what he's preparing to do—fling his body over his head to land on his back— seems extraordinarily difficult and dangerous. He extrapolates that there will be a moment, mid-"somersault," when the only body parts touching the ground will be his fingertips and his skull. This seems like a pretty advanced gymnastic maneuver. What he knows of somersaults is that they are simple, joyous, carefree exercises, very basic tumbling, and so he knows he is getting something wrong. Kneeling, with his forehead on

8

the carpet, Abbott is certain this is not a somersault but considers going through with it anyway, in the spirit of fun physical play. "Chipmunk!" his daughter shouts. Abbott's wife enters and says, "Oooh, Dad's trying a somersault. Careful, Dad." "Dad do it," his daughter says, suddenly re-engaged. Abbott remembers the feeling of climbing up to the high dive at the county pool. You couldn't very well climb back down the ladder. "This is a somersault?" he asks, forehead on carpet. "What do *you* think it is?" his wife says. "Is she watching?" he asks. "You know, sort of," she says. So then he goes through with it, a dizzying and undisciplined tumble, concluding in mild nausea and a grunt. Less a roll than an accidental fall. His breath is ragged as he stares at the ceiling. The pain, Abbott thinks, might be his kidney. His wife and daughter clap and laugh. "You've got to tuck your chin, sweetheart," his wife says. A man does not always know his ultimate acts—the last time he swims in the ocean, the last time he makes love. But at age thirty-seven, perhaps the midpoint of his one and only life, Abbott knows that he has attempted his final somersault.

3 Abbott and the Inoperative Traffic Light

After a violent thunderstorm rumbles through the Pioneer Valley, bending the maples and traumatizing the family dog, Abbott leaves his house to buy an ink cartridge for his printer. While driving, he notices the large tree branches in the yards and streets. He hears sirens in the distance. The sun is out now, and the wet asphalt steams. As Abbott approaches a busy four-way intersection, he observes that the light is inoperative, knocked out, presumably, by the storm. There is no police officer directing the traffic. With a button he locks the doors of his car. He is reminded of his insufficient life-insurance policy. Gradually, however, he perceives what is happening at the intersection ahead. The drivers, as if by prior agreement, are treating this broken traffic light as a four-way stop, and they are *taking turns* moving through. If Abbott is not mistaken, there is a coordinated counterclockwise movement to the turn-taking. Occasionally there are pauses during which no car ventures forth, but then one motorist will signal to another, who then waves and proceeds. Everyone is using appropriate signals. Abbott has witnessed this kind of egalitarian poststorm automotive subcommunity two or three other times in his life, and each time it has nearly brought him to tears. The rip in the social order neatly mended by a group of morally imaginative and mutually supporting human drivers with a firm and instinctual sense of fairness. Here's a repudiation of Thomas Hobbes, William Golding, Abbott's father. When Abbott stops in front of the broken light, he signals a middle-aged Asian man to go ahead and make the right turn the Asian man has indicated he would like to make. (The Asian man turns right and waves.) Abbott looks at the motorist to his left. A woman who appears to be a yoga instructor waggles her fingers above her steering wheel, beckoning forth Abbott, who waves ardently as he passes straight through the intersection on the way to buy the ink cartridge for his printer. The graded streets and the storm drains are doing their work. The sun is bright and cleansing. All the college kids are gone. This should be the end of the story, but it isn't. At the end of the story, which is right now, Abbott is thinking once more about what happened to that baby in Tulsa.

4 Abbott's Dog

Abbott's dog is a sturdy, fit, and handsome yellow Lab that just might be, pound for pound, God's most timorous creation. The dog has always been terribly afraid of thunder, fireworks, and backfiring engines, but the scope and intensity of his fear have increased as he has aged. At eleven, he now fears airplanes, garbage trucks, delivery vans, other dogs, cats, people, loud birds and bugs, scarecrows, snowmen, kites and flags, some trees, heavy rain, light rain, fog, cloudy skies, partly cloudy skies, gusts of wind, refreshing summer breezes. Also, he seems scared of what can most accurately be described as *nothing*. The symptoms of his fear include violent trembling, panting, shedding, and drooling so excessive that his front paws become shiny and slick. Abbott's wife frequently says that the animal *senses* barometric shifts, distant weather phenomena. "No, he doesn't," Abbott says. Each night for the past week Abbott's dog has been, for no discernible reason, overthrown by fright. Abbott's wife, in her third trimester, is up frequently to urinate. Upon her return to bed, Abbott has noticed the dog shaking and attempting to get beneath things far too small to get beneath, his bad breath disseminated by panting. "There must be a storm moving in," Abbott's wife says, nightly. Abbott has yanked open the blinds to point out what he thinks is the Little Dipper. "Look," he has said for a week. "There's no storm." "It's far off," his wife has said. "He can sense it." Now tonight, after five or six stormless nights, Abbott, uncomfortable with mystery and irritated with the dog, strives to detect in the night some fear-inducing pulse or wave during his wife's brief trip to the bathroom down the hall. He sits up in bed, holds his breath, cocks his head receptively, and in this way he achieves a promising hypothesis: The dog seems terrified by the barely audible rumble of unrolling toilet paper. This conjecture, Abbott knows, requires a well-designed experiment and a willing assistant. He entreats his wife to remove, so very quietly, the toilet-paper roll from its wall-mounted holder the next time she urinates. Once she has removed the roll she can—Abbott's wife says she can handle it from there. When the time comes, about two hours later, she executes the test with a proficiency that compensates for her poor attitude. Meanwhile, Abbott observes the dog with rigor and dispassion. He notes that the subject, while markedly anxious about Abbott's wife's absence, does not exhibit the symptoms of a full-blown fear-based episode. The nonoccurrence of terror seems to confirm the hypothesis (though Abbott feels compelled to run a few more trials, both with and without the wall-mounted holder). This is a story Abbott would like to tell colleagues at a faculty cocktail party, should he ever attend one. It can be enjoyed as a humorous and suspenseful anecdote about a family pet, and it can also be enjoyed as a parable of the Enlightenment. Abbott imagines the clustered scholars leaning into his story, their cocktails nearly spilling onto the dean's rug. To enhance the narrative's dramatic effects—and to tease out its lofty implications about knowledge formation—Abbott finds that he must take small liberties with the truth. He embellishes, amplifies. He omits. For instance, Abbott sees no reason to tell the captivated imaginary gathering that his typical response to the dog's fear is not sympathy or even intellectual curiosity but anger and exasperation. It drives Abbott *crazy* that the dog continually becomes so distraught over so little, and that the animal cannot, when afraid, be placated by words, logic, evidence, affection, or cheese. Best not to mention any of this, Abbott knows, but it's so galling, all that hair in the closet, the drool on the floor. Here is a creature that understands from Abbott's *choice of shoes* that it's time for a walk, yet refuses to comprehend that a birthday balloon is not a mortal threat. Now, abruptly, Abbott's story is gone, supplanted by the anger and exasperation he removed from it. He does not know—he can't be certain—why he is so angered and exasperated by the dog's stubborn fearfulness. Abbott's wife's hypothesis is, Abbott maintains, unverifiable.

5 In Which Abbott Is Surprised by Artifice

As it turns out, a well-known actress's tears in a well-known movie are not real tears. They are a special effect, added after shooting. The director, called out by some heroic entertainment watchdog organization, defends the actress in an interview, saying she could have cried real tears had she been asked to. She was not asked to. She's a fine actress, deserving of an Academy Award. It was only when the director was editing that he decided her crying would improve the scene in question. So, yes, he digitally inserted some tears. He does not understand the controversy. After all, the car chase in the movie is not real, nor is the triple homicide. On the Internet there is a still from the movie of the crying actress, and Abbott notices that the tears really do look fake—big, round, firm Hollywood orbs, dewdrops on a morning leaf. They look like they could stream upward, climb the actress's face. The director says in the interview that let's not forget art is an illusion. He says that even had the actress's tears been real, they would have been fake. He says just think about it. Abbott understands why Plato kicked these guys out of his city. "What they should do," Abbott says at the dinner table, ostensibly to his wife, the only other adult present, "is put tears on everyone's faces in every movie. Comedy, action, drama. Everyone. Every character in every movie, weeping from the opening credits to the end. What scene would not be improved? That's what I'd like to see. That's what they should do." Most evenings they sit down together as a family for dinner, usually about 4:45. "It's difficult," Abbott's wife says to Abbott after a while, "to have a relationship with the entire world." Their daughter says, "More cucumber?" His wife says, "Do you know what I mean?" Abbott thinks he does know what she means. What she means, he thinks, is it's impossible. What she means is, Please knock it off. Don't just leave the table as soon as you finish your dinner. Live with us, here, now, in this house.

6 Abbott and the Paradox of Personal Growth

Abbott has two hours and fifteen minutes of child care before his wife takes over. He and his daughter take a hot morning walk around the neighborhood at a gruelingly slow pace, returning home with quite a few acorns and a flat gray rock. Abbott prepares himself before checking the clock in the kitchen. He estimates the time by subtracting fifteen minutes from his most conservative estimate of the time, but then discovers that he is still ten minutes fast. The morning yawns before him. He reads a book to her six times in a row, wanting very much to set the author's house on fire. The girl spills juice on the carpet, and Abbott blots it with his shirt. They look at a neighbor's cat in the yard. They ruin a yoyo. They spin a propeller. They eat animal crackers. They play with a long-necked toy dinosaur whose wonderful scientific name, Abbott will learn later, has secretly been changed to a name not nearly so good. Abbott looks at the clock and calls out in pain. His four-and-a-half cups of coffee have been, according to the calibration on the pot, eleven cups of coffee. They make Remote Control dance. They find a ladybug, some brown pine needles that must have fallen from the Christmas tree. They sort beads by color, by size. They roll the beads down inclined surfaces. "Dad sit right here," Abbott's daughter says, and Abbott sits right there. "Hold this," she says, and he holds it. "Do this," she says, and he does it. "Not like that," she says. What did Abbott used to do with his summer mornings? He cannot even remember, cannot contemplate the freedom, the terrible enormity of Self. Abbott's wife walks into the family room and kisses his warm head and his daughter's warm head. Then she sits on the floor in a playing position. Abbott gulps the rest of his tepid coffee and goes to bed. He can hear his wife and his daughter talking at the dining-room table. "What do you think we should name the baby?" Abbott's wife asks. There is a pause before the girl says, "Cheetah." Abbott approaches sleep with an ineffable sense of relief that he did not know, before having a child, what it was like to have a child—did not *really* know what it was *really* like—because if he had known before having a child how profoundly strenuous and self-obliterating it is to have a child, he never would have had a child, and then, or now, he would not have this remarkable child. Abbott's wife, were she here, might say that it doesn't quite make sense. Abbott might rub her hip lightly with the back of his hand. "That's the thing," he might say.

7 Abbott's Dread

It can happen at any time, in any room of the house. Abbott is never safe, and neither, consequently, is his wife. This afternoon, as Abbott kneels in the kitchen, pouring kibble from a forty-pound bag into a plastic bin from which the dog is fed, a folded coupon falls to the tile floor, frightening the dog. The coupon is covered in a fine coating of kibble dust. Unconcerned, Abbott picks it up and hands it to his wife, who is in charge of coupons. "Here," he says, unaware that it is a smuggled and coded message. She unfolds the coupon to determine its value and its restrictions. She snorts. "This expires in *2017*," she says. Abbott looks up from his task, spilling some kibble across the floor. He feels an unpleasant tingle at the back of his neck. Will there be dog food in 2017? Or grocery stores? Or legal tender? "Ever notice," Abbott says to his wife's back, "that when you say a future year out loud, it sounds kind of ominous?" The dog eats the hearty nuggets one by one from the floor. Abbott says, "Not when you see them written, but when you say them out loud. 2023. 2048. The plan is to cut carbon emissions in half by 2051. Congratulations to the class of 2040." His wife says, "Let me try. Wait. OK. The treaty expires in 2074." Abbott nods. "*See?*" he says.

8 Wonderful Life

The Internet, Abbott reads tonight on the Internet, is now believed by
experts to be one percent pornography. Somewhere, no doubt, confetti
settles onto tumid organs. When Abbott browses the Internet, he imagines all that porn lurking inside the monitor, directly behind the screen
he is browsing. It's *in* there, it's in his computer. Just a flimsy scrim of
tragic news headlines dropped between his torpid gaze and all that nudity
and unorthodox penetration. He imagines that one small transposition of
letters in a Web address will produce a beaver, an anus, someone peeing
on someone else. This thought, like so much of American life, renders
him titillated and despondent. Abbott is not a prude about porn. Or,
to put it another way, he is a prude about porn. He just wonders if the
consumption of pornography can legitimately be considered a component
of human flourishing. All that loneliness and credit-card debt. The thesis
of Stephen Jay Gould's *Wonderful Life* is that humans are an entity, not
a tendency. "We are a thing, an item of history," Gould writes, "not an
embodiment of general principles." After a thorough analysis of the
530-million-year-old fossil record in a limestone quarry called the Burgess

Shale—and of the mass extinctions of species that occurred after the quarry was formed—Gould concludes that the evolution of human life was spectacularly unlikely, a lottery win. "Replay the tape a million times from a Burgess beginning," Gould argues, "and I doubt that anything like *Homo sapiens* would ever evolve again." With great mental exertion and a decent night's sleep and no ambient noise, Abbott can hold this concept precariously in his mind, like an acrobat balancing a chair holding a sequined assistant. But when he tries, in his mind, to add the proliferation of Internet pornography to Gould's thesis on historical contingency, the strain becomes too much and he nearly blacks out in titillation and despondency. What an awful miracle. Abbott knows from Keats that the fancy thing to do is to reside in Paradox *without any irritable reaching*. But he also knows that he is, above all else, an irritable reacher, and about as capable of reform as a trembling dog. (There is rain on the roof, song on the monitor. He could just type in *wild sluts*, get it over with.)

9 Abbott's Imaginary Letter to an Imaginary Nationally Syndicated Childhood and Parenting Expert

Here's one for the Puzzled Parents mailbag. Most mornings, Abbott explains, he gets up early with his young daughter while his wife, a pregnant insomniac, tries to sleep in. He prepares breakfast for his child and then sits with her at the table while she eats. Well, it *is* nice time together, but the truth is that Abbott on most mornings is listless and taciturn. Sometimes—understand that it is very early and there is no nanny and he's so *tired* and it seems increasingly unlikely that he will ever be consulted for a fascinating story on public radio—he has his head in his hands. The girl eats and chatters across the table while Abbott grinds his eyeballs with his palms. But occasionally, and for reasons he doesn't understand, Abbott is fun and funny at breakfast. He makes faces and voices, he hides behind cereal boxes, he pretends to spit out bad-tasting food, he flaps his arms and flies around the table. Hold on, he's getting to his question. Abbott's daughter loves it when this strange father appears, though she can never depend on his appearance. Abbott is troubled by his inconsistency. He knows that a parent's consistency is vital, that children thrive when they feel a sense of steadiness and reliability at home. His question, then, is whether he should desist with the infrequent jollity and just be consistently sullen and unresponsive at breakfast. He is Yours Sincerely, Piqued in the Valley.

10 Abbott and the Jacobite Revolts

Abbott sits on the edge of his daughter's bed after she wakes from a long nap. The girl is happy and full of song. "My body," she sings, clapping her hands. Her fingers are splayed and so extended as to bend slightly back, so that only her palms touch when she claps. "My body, my body," she sings. She looks to Abbott both tiny and enormous lying beneath her sheet. She is flushed and sweaty. "Dad," she says. "My body, my body." Abbott does not know where she learned this song. "It does sound like *body*," he says. "It does." His daughter sings, "My body, my body." "It does sound like that," he says. "But it's Bonnie." His daughter sings, "My body, my body." Abbott says, "It does sound like that, honey, but it's Bonnie. Bonnie. Bonnie." His daughter says, "Dad." "Like an *nnnnnnn* sound," he says. "Bonnie." His daughter claps her palms and sings a jumbled line about the sea. Abbott sings:

> My Bonnie lies over the ocean
> My Bonnie lies over the sea
> My Bonnie lies over the ocean
> Oh bring back my Bonnie to me

Abbott's daughter says, "Be careful, Popo." She makes her stuffed pony climb the wall. Quietly she sings, "My body, my body."
Abbott moves to the refrain:

> Bring back bring back
> Oh bring back my Bonnie to me, to me
> Bring back, bring back
> Oh bring back my Bonnie to me

Abbott's daughter says, "Open the window?" Abbott gets up and opens the blinds. "It's light up," she says. "Yes," he says. "Sunny out," she says, even though it clearly isn't. Abbott commences the second verse, which he did not even know he knew until he was singing it:

> Last night as I lay on my pillow
> Last night as I lay on my bed
> Last night as I lay on my pillow
> I dreamt that my Bonnie was dead

Abbott swallows the last word. Who taught his daughter this Scottish folk song about Charles Edward Stuart ("Bonnie Prince Charlie"), who in 1745, after two decades of exile in Italy, returned to his homeland to regain the English throne for his family, only to be routed by the Redcoats and forced to escape the country disguised as a servant girl? Not that she learned it all that well, but still. He sings the chorus one more time, dramatically. He's trying to win back his daughter's attention because she has scrambled down the bed and is flipping through a book about a coyote. "My body, my body," she sings. "*Nnnnnn,*" says Abbott, who in all honesty has a spotty grasp of English monarchical rule and who does not until twenty minutes later conduct Internet research on the song's origins while ignoring the girl's demands for grapes. "It's about really missing a lady who is gone," he misinforms his daughter, who is running away from him and down the hallway, "and who may have suffered some kind of misfortune on the water . . ." Later that night in bed, Abbott's wife, aggrievedly not asleep, says she simply cannot stand children's music and that she will go insane—and she really means insane—if she doesn't cleanse from her mind this detestable song featured on one of their daughter's new CDs. Abbott can empathize. He has had trapped in his skull for the past twenty minutes a vaguely tragic but ultimately unintelligible song called "Hinky Dinky Dee." His wife thrashes the sheets. "Here it is," she says. "I'm giving it to you." She sings a frantic refrain:

> My body my body
> My body can do lots of things
> Look at me don't you see I can move so easily
> My body my body

11 Abbott and the Highchair

Abbott is out in his driveway washing his daughter's highchair with a
hose, a sponge, and a soapy bucket. Neighbors walk by and say boy do
they remember those days. They say he can wash their cars when he's
done. They say he should start a small business. The neighbors stop with
their leashed dogs and tell stories of rotting fruit and yogurt beneath the
seat cushions, the mysterious stenches, the revolting discoveries. Oh they
don't miss that. Abbott says these highchairs really do get disgusting.
The neighbors say they literally gagged. You just don't understand it, they
say, until you have children. I know, says Abbott, it's bad. One woman
whose name Abbott thinks is Laura says her husband is taking it easy
for a couple days after the vasectomy. Abbott changes the setting on his
new hose attachment from SHOWER to JET, and he blasts the highchair
so hard it rocks back on two plastic wheels. Desiccated raisins fly like
shrapnel. A small, personal rainbow glistens in the mist at the face of the
new hose attachment.

12 Abbott Hogs the Mood

Like many others before him, Abbott discovers, once married, that marriage is a battle—clinically, a *negotiation*—over the possession of the Bad Mood. A marriage, especially a marriage with children, cannot function properly if both its constituents are in foul temper, thus the Bad Mood is a privilege only one spouse can enjoy at a time. Who gets to be in a Bad Mood? This is the day-to-day struggle. In the Perfect Union, the Bad Mood is traded equitably, like child care or household chores. There is joint custody of the Bad Mood. If one spouse is grumpy for an entire weekend, the other spouse might take the Mood for the workweek. If one spouse is low-spirited during that unpleasant stretch from Christmas to the New Year, the other spouse might claim Thanksgiving, Easter, and the Fourth of July. In the typical marriage, however, one spouse tends to possess the Bad Mood disproportionately. This is called Hogging the Mood. Abbott peacefully acquired his wife's Bad Mood in a long line at the Big Y during a late afternoon last February, a Thursday, and he has not given it up in four months. It is a testament to his wife's good nature that she did not, initially, try to reclaim the Mood, as she had every right to do. She is pregnant, after all, and sleeping poorly. For the first few weeks, even a month, she let Abbott have it, no questions asked. Like a friendly librarian, she has always had a lenient overdue policy, and besides, Abbott suspects they have a tacit understanding that he requires the Bad Mood slightly more than she does. Although they have never kept a record—at least he hasn't—he is reasonably certain that he has been majority owner of the Bad Mood during the marriage. Also, he supposes that she imagines there will be some attractive mood compensation package for her patience and goodwill. But as the weeks and months pass, Abbott senses that she is growing anxious to repossess the Bad Mood. She tries sex, and she tries withholding sex. She tries lighthearted humor and then lighthearted threat. We can, she says, do this the hard way or the easy way. She says broken kneecaps. Eventually she employs guerrilla tactics, surprise raids, quick and deep mood plunges designed to buoy Abbott's mood and achieve marital equilibrium. But he holds fast. He wants the Bad Mood—he feels he needs it—and giving it up after holding it so long begins to seem arbitrary. He has had it this long—why cede it now? Many times he feels himself veering close to enjoyment or contentment, but then, realizing the risk, he retreats to the center of the Mood. And then this afternoon Abbott returns home from the hardware store and sees his young daughter running out to the driveway to meet him. She says "Dad" over and over again, grabs his leg like a child in an advertisement for life insurance or home mortgage. She smiles up at him, jumping, chanting "Dad," as if he has been a good father. Abbott kneels to pick her up. He puts his arms around her neck and whispers something affectionate into her ear. Her curly hair tickles his face. When he looks up, he sees his wife watching them from the kitchen window, and that's when he loses it.

13 Abbott Suffers the Pang of Vindication

Here in the corner of the basement, searching in and among cardboard boxes for a paint tray and rollers, Abbott finds the water. Six gallons, perhaps not *hidden*, but certainly *stashed*. His initial confusion gives way to satisfaction, which gives way to disturbance. This is not an argument one wishes to win. As long as Abbott's wife is nonchalant about apocalypse, as long as her arguments derive from unexamined notions of hope and progress, as long as she does not surreptitiously buy emergency supplies, the household can exist in a delicate but sustainable balance. *He's* the one who fears the cataclysmic demise of Western Civilization, not her. But now this dreadful evidence, this unwelcome glimpse inside her. How difficult to know someone, and how undesirable. Six gallons. Abbott walks across the basement to check on the three gallons he has hidden in the opposite corner. There they are, beneath a broken trampoline, looking insufficient. He wonders if she is twice as scared or just twice as diligent.

14 In Which Abbott Fails to Complete a Pretty Basic Task

When Abbott comes in from mowing, he finds his wife cutting his daughter's hair in the middle of the kitchen. The girl is sitting in her highchair with a towel around her shoulders. She holds still; her face is grave, stoic. Abbott's wife is biting her lip in concentration. She is using the family's one pair of scissors, which is also used to cut paper, cardboard, fabric, wire, rubber, rope, dog-food bags, plastic packages of batteries, and once, in the middle of the night, aluminum. "I didn't know you were going to do this," Abbott says, wiping the sweat from his face and neck with a paper towel. Abbott's wife mists the girl's hair with a spray bottle Abbott has never seen before, not once. Abbott feels like an interloper. He tries to fade to the dark perimeter of the small kitchen, but there isn't one. "When did you learn how to do that?" he says. Abbott's wife leans down and closes one eye to check if the back of the girl's hair is even. She's so capable, so confident. So skilled and courageous with her dull scissors. "It's not like I *know how*," she says. "I'm just doing it." The ring of locks around the girl's highchair looks to Abbott ceremonial or ritualistic. Abbott would no sooner cut his daughter's hair than remove her appendix. He has never even considered that her hair would need to be cut, but of course her hair needs to be cut. What is the appropriate response to your daughter's first haircut? Why is he sad and afraid? Abbott's wife makes one more tiny snip and then circles the highchair, gently pulling strands of the girl's hair. "There," she says. "That looks great." Abbott nods. It does look good. He emerges into the center of the room and puts his hand on the girl's head. "No, Dad," she says. "Would you mind sweeping up this hair?" his wife asks. Abbott slinks to the closet for the broom and the thing that you sweep things into. "Do you want to see?" Abbott's wife says to their daughter, holding up a mirror. Abbott sweeps the hair into the thing and holds it. Golden ringlets is what they are. "What am I supposed to do with this?" he says. His wife says, "Just toss it." Abbott walks to the trash can, opens the lid, and sees the coffee grounds, a leathery carrot, some wet noodles, and a diaper. He closes the lid. Abbott's wife holds the mirror, brushes loose hair from the girl's neck. "Well," she says, "why don't you take it outside and spread it to the winds?" Abbott says, "Really?" "It's an organic substance," his wife says. Abbott takes his daughter's hair outside. He walks through the pachysandra and onto the lawn, smelling the cut grass and exhaust. The cat dashes across the yard, reminding Abbott that he has a cat. The birds are making a racket in the trees, and Abbott squints up into bright sun. Then he looks back down at the golden hair against the green plastic. He walks back through the pachysandra and into the house. His wife and daughter have moved to some other room. He can hear their voices. From a kitchen drawer he takes a sandwich bag. He pours in the hair, seals the bag, and places it behind a cookbook on top of the refrigerator, where it will remain either forever or until Abbott's wife removes it.

15 The Expatriate

Parenthood is a distant and peculiar country with its own customs and language. To people not living in Parenthood, the citizens of Parenthood may sound as if they have suffered an injury to a small but significant sector of the brain. "These are not the sensitive wipes!" Abbott's wife shouts from their daughter's bedroom. "And all these books in here *really* need to be washed." "*Hey!*" Abbott hollers. "Why did you erase Blue Robot?"

16 Abbott and the Wrong Tool

Abbott is embarrassed about his broom. It is not, he knows, the right tool for the job. Abbott in his adult years has accumulated a fair number of tools, almost all of which happen not to be the right tool for the job. Abbott saw his neighbors—months ago, at the first buds of spring—sweep the snowplowed rocks from their front lawns to the street with large indoor/outdoor push brooms. These things had rubber grips, hardy bristles, lifetime warranties. Abbott's broom is a standard straw kitchen model, and it isn't doing much to chase the gravel from the crabgrass. He imagines an assembly of Pilgrims watching him from the street and shaking their heads. Abbott knows he should purchase the correct broom but in doing so he feels that he will commit himself entirely to this house, this lawn, this neighborhood, this family, this economic status, this climate, this region and its unfamiliar cycles—the winter plows, the spring sweeps, the seasonal relocation of gravel. If he owns the broom, then he will be sweeping this weedy yard each year until his death. The improper broom is embarrassing, but it keeps Abbott's options open. He can enjoy the freedom of the dabbler, though it is true that he is not enjoying his afternoon on the lawn. To brush the rocks from the grass and weeds, he must use an incredibly forceful raking motion, and soon his wrists and forearms are sore, and he is, he notices, developing blisters on his hands. There are gloves in the garage, but they are the wrong kind. Abbott takes a break. He cannot lean on his broom, and he does not smoke cigarettes. The tall banks of clouds to the east look like a kingdom moving in. Or to the west. A Japanese neighbor hangs wet clothes on the line. What happened this morning is that Abbott spoke loudly at his daughter. This loud speaking might in fact have been yelling. The girl was imploring—Abbott does not remember about what—and he spoke loudly at her. He said, "Stop it." He exclaimed. "You just push and push and *push*," he said to her. "You will not let up." Abbott knows that parents should not yell, that yelling just makes things worse and teaches children to yell. He knows he should maintain at all times a calm and controlled voice. He knows he should praise good behavior and simply ignore bad behavior until it disappears forever. Abbott can see that the broom is disintegrating. Pieces of straw are now mixed in with the gravel, and their extraction will require the use of some tool he does not own. It's bad enough that he yelled at the child. What's far worse is that his outburst to the two-year-old was nearly verbatim what Abbott had said several nights earlier, less loudly but more viciously, to his wife. He realized this as he said the words this morning, heard them, felt the familiar plosion of the *push and push and push*. There are different ways to articulate his misconduct, different angles of prosecution. It's demeaning, Abbott suspects, to speak to your wife in the same way that you speak to your young daughter, while it might be downright creepy to speak to your young daughter in the same way that you speak to your wife. In either case, it means that Abbott has acted as if he is married to a toddler. But Abbott takes comfort in the suspicion that the problem is actually much more dire and generalized, not particular to his wife and daughter. He might, he thinks, yell these words at anyone, anything, in his small beseeching world. There is nothing that won't not let up. Every day these cadgers and supplicants—the broken hinge, the moldy tub, the dog who has to pee. Down the street, coming closer, that sweaty college kid, collecting signatures for cleaner air.

17 Father's Day

It's already hot at 8:36 when Abbott and his daughter squat down beside the runoff grate at the edge of the road in front of their house. The girl says, "Rocks." Abbott picks up three small rocks, puts them in his palm, and extends his palm toward his daughter. His daughter pinches a rock between her thumb and forefinger, then holds it over the grate a moment before dropping it in. Abbott and his daughter listen for the sound of the rock hitting water—a faint, high-pitched *bloop* that reverberates in the dark tunnel. The girl laughs when she hears it. Abbott extends his palm again, and his daughter pinches a rock and drops it into the grate, laughing when the rock hits water. Abbott offers the last rock, and the girl takes it and drops it into the grate, but the rock is too small and flat to produce a sound. The girl holds still for several seconds, waiting for the noise. Then she says, "More rocks?" Abbott is uncomfortable in his squat. He has begun having pain in his right hip. He of course considers arthritis. He picks up three more rocks, puts them in his palm, and extends his palm toward his daughter. A spry, gray-haired man, either a full professor or a retired full professor, walks up to the grate and stops.

"My kids used to love putting rocks in that damn grate thirty years ago," he says to Abbott. "Every kid in this neighborhood has dropped rocks in that grate. Decades of rocks. It's a wonder the tunnel isn't all clogged up." The man's tone, a complex blend of sympathy and severity, is a unique characteristic of the region and still perplexing to Abbott, who grew up with the comforts of superficial nicety. Abbott knows not whether to feel consoled that he is part of a lineage or irritated that his hardship is so prosaic. "Have a good day," Abbott says to the man. Abbott's daughter says, "Man." With her thumb and forefinger she pinches a rock out of Abbott's extended palm, holds the rock tantalizingly above the grate, then drops it. She smiles when she hears the reverberant *bloop*. She says, "Bloop." She pinches another rock from Abbott's hand, holds it above the grate, drops it. The rock, when it hits the water, makes a faint, high-pitched sound that echoes softly in the dark tunnel. "More rocks?" the girl says. "Here's another one," Abbott says, extending his palm. It's 8:39, hot. Somewhere a mower is already buzzing. Abbott comes out of his squat and sits on the road beside the grate. A neighbor drives by and waves. There are dozens, if not hundreds, of small rocks within Abbott's reach. The girl drops the rock in the grate, smiles when she hears the noise. "More rocks?" she says. A dog barks in some backyard. A cloud covers and then uncovers the sun. Campus is distant and theoretical, like a galaxy or heaven. There is something beyond tedium. You can pass all the way through tedium and come out the other side, and this is Abbott's gift today. He picks up a pinecone, puts it in his palm, and extends his palm toward his daughter. The girl's eyes grow wide and she laughs. She reaches for the pinecone, says, "Pinecone."

18 All Observation, Darwin Noted, Must Be For or Against Some View If It Is to Be of Any Service

Abbott would like to think he's a *good guy,* and yet his wife is up there sobbing, and he's down here with the superglue.

19 Abbott's Mind

Abbott nearly swerves into a mailbox trying to read the church's hand-lettered advertisement for a forthcoming sermon entitled TOLERANCE IS NOT THE SAME AS LOVE. There is no need for comment or response. No need, even, for thought. Abbott knows that you are supposed to envision your mind, your consciousness, as a clean and empty room, open windows on opposite walls, the wind just passing through. The wind is the world, here and gone, or perhaps only here. Abbott likes to add white fluttering curtains to give the wind form, but he soon discovers that the room of his consciousness has a curtain rod, some hardware, a cordless drill with a battery that needs to be charged. He'll need an electrical outlet. Is the room wired? He can't remember what the things on the ends of curtain rods are called. They have a name. The wind swirls in his room, stirring up dust. Abbott has thoughts, he can't help it, about the hand-lettered advertisement for the sermon. One thought is that tolerance, while admittedly not identical to love, is, on an imaginary Continuum of Regard, a good deal closer to love than enriched uranium. Another thought, buried beneath the first like an earthquake survivor, is that there is in fact not one thing the same as love, including love.

20 Malaise Is for Renters

Some stories, like this one, have more than one ending. Here is the beginning: When his family moved into the house in Western Massachusetts, Abbott found an old nine-by-twelve carpet rolled against a wall in the unfinished basement. Soon after settling in, Abbott unrolled the musty but serviceable carpet on the cement floor. He then placed the cat's litter box atop the carpet, both to create a comfortable excretory environment for the cat and to limit the dispersal of litter. During the winter, Abbott began to suspect the cat was spraying the carpet, but the carpet is dark and the basement lighting is poor, and he did not care to investigate the matter. When spring arrived with higher temperatures and higher humidity, however, the basement began to reek. And then tonight, Abbott, dizzy with the fumes, investigates the matter and realizes with a cold shudder that the carpet is soaked with cat piss that apparently never dries. Not dealing with it is no longer an option. He must put his hands on the carpet, and now. Abbott rolls the carpet (wincing at the wet cement beneath), opens the rusted metal doors of the bulkhead, and drags the sodden, cylindrical load up six wooden stairs to the backyard, then around the house to the driveway. Now is the time for thinking. The carpet is far too big to leave by the curb for the weekly garbage pickup, and also too big to place in or on his car to take to the dump. Abbott knows what must be done, and he selects from his garage a standard carpentry saw, with which he attempts to cut a strip from the carpet along the twelve-foot side. The carpet, however, has a thick border, reinforced, Abbott will come to learn, by saw-resistant wire. Thus he returns to the garage and emerges with a large pair of hedge clippers, and with some effort he manages to slice the carpet's border. The word Abbott cannot quite remember until much later is *selvage*. The sun has dipped below the tops of the big trees, but the night is still quite hot, and Abbott is sweating. The windows of his house are open, and he can hear his wife tell his daughter, "No mouth." Once he has sliced through the carpet's border with the hedge clippers, he is able, with considerable exertion, to cut a nine-foot strip with the saw, stopping at the bottom border to use the hedge clippers again. With this combination of tools, he makes seven long cuts, creating eight strips of filthy, urinous carpet, nine feet long and roughly eighteen inches wide. This takes quite a while. The wire inside the carpet borders cuts his fingers, which are wet with piss and slimy nuggets of cat litter. He hears his wife tell his daughter, "Time for your bath." Neighbors walk by and watch him cut carpet with a saw. It is possible, he knows, that they can smell the ammonia from the street. He does not look up, does not indicate that he is available for chitchat. Even so, they call out, "Looks like you got your hands full there," and, "What you need is a carpet cutter." He grunts assent, wipes his brow with his sweaty shirt. Abbott rolls each of the eight nine-foot strips into a tight, damp bundle, and he stacks the bundles in the driveway like firewood. *Cord,* he thinks. He hears his wife tell his daughter, "Let's get you to bed." He returns the hedge clippers and saw to the garage, and he sweeps up the litter and carpet fluff from the driveway. Then he takes from the garage an empty plastic garbage can and a box of heavy-duty lawn bags. He places the carpet rolls in two bags, four to a bag, and he heaves the bags into the garbage can. He tries to push the lid on, but it will not fit. That one vivid star must be Venus. Garbage pickup, Abbott remembers, is not tomorrow but the following day. He would rather the stuffed and lidless can not sit incriminatingly at the street for thirty-six hours, so he decides to drag it back into the garage. This kind of dragging will eventually wear a hole in the bottom of the can, but Abbott does not know that yet, and he is untroubled. He presses an illuminated doorbell button mounted on a two-by-four, and the garage door drops slowly like a final curtain. And this is where the story furcates like lightning, strikes ground in four places. The first ending is about Ernest Hemingway and masculinity: catching speckled trout in a cold stream, knocking them dead on a flat rock, furling them in leaves, and placing them in a shady spot until dinner. The second ending is cold and familiar, another variation of the look-behind-the-refrigerator horror of domesticity and the soul-diminishing obligations of middle-class citizenship. The third ending is a virulent eco-sci-fi scenario, involving planetary visitors in the year 2820 who find massive underground deposits of nondegraded carpet. The fourth ending is the riskiest and the most interesting. This ending makes a sincere attempt at Franklinian homily, and it goes more or less like this: Almost any task, no matter how initially abhorrent, can, if conceived with Ingenuity and executed with Industry, create feelings of Satisfaction and Pleasure.

21 Abbott and the Longest Day of the Year

Amidst the toys in the family room is a battery-operated light-sensitive jungle-animal-sounds puzzle, given to Abbott's daughter either by a childless friend of Abbott or a friend of Abbott who hates Abbott. Tonight, like all the nights, Abbott and his wife clean the family room after putting their daughter to bed. Tonight, like all the nights, when they turn off the light after cleaning they activate a loud light-sensitive jungle-animal sound—an unspecifically savage squawk from the bottom of the puzzle crate. A monkey, perhaps, or parrot. Tonight, like all the nights, the jungle-animal sound is an agonizing surprise, an ambush. Abbott and his wife laugh and say curse words. *Shit* and *fuck*, for instance. The imprecations, because they are directed at a puzzle for children ages two to four, seem more vulgar and thus more satisfying. Tonight, like all the nights, Abbott says he will just take the batteries out of that motherfucker. Outside, the sun is setting, and the sky has turned that color that is both lovely and frightening. "Yeah, yeah, yeah," says Abbott's wife, vanishing down the dark hallway. This day, like all the days, endless and gone.

22 The Abbott Hubcap Index (AHI)

As Abbott drives homeward through the Pioneer Valley, his spirits are lifted by the sight of a shining hubcap propped against a maple tree, and then another against a weathered wooden fence. They look like gleaming medals bestowed upon the human race. The probability of a driver ever locating a missing hubcap is remote, of course, which is precisely what makes hubcap-propping such a poignant act. These anonymous pedestrians have propped hubcaps because they know if they ever lost a hubcap, they would want someone else to prop it. It's the foundation of all moral philosophy. Then, as Abbott nears his house, he notices his neighbor has returned home from a weeklong trip in his new car. He notices, furthermore, that the wheels on the driver's side are missing their hubcaps. The car, so sleek just days ago, now looks dilapidated. Considering the possibility of a design flaw, Abbott drives around the block in order to examine the car's passenger side, and he observes then that those hubcaps are also missing. Whatever he might wish to believe, Abbott knows it is statistically unlikely that all four hubcaps fell off this new car. He stops just past his neighbor's driveway, stares back into the black nothingness at the center of the tires. He feels that he is within a drama of contending moral forces, as we find in Hawthorne. Is it unreasonable, Abbott wonders, to want to live and raise children in a land where the number of propped hubcaps (PH) exceeds the number of stolen hubcaps (SH)? He imagines a list of industrialized nations, ranked according to a hubcap index—the ratio *PH:SH*, expressed as the average number of propped hubcaps per one stolen hubcap. An index of 2 would be righteous indeed. Really, anything above 1 would be an index of virtue, as it would indicate that the citizens' noblest instincts were prevailing, by however slight a margin. The USA, Abbott speculates, certainly has an index no greater than the 0.5 he has recorded this afternoon. Sweden's ratio is probably the best. Sweden's or Norway's.

23 Abbott RSVPs

Regretfully, again, Abbott cannot attend. The timing is inopportune. Checking his calendar, Abbott finds that he has a prior engagement on the day in question. On that day, he needs to rise early with his daughter to play in the family room with buttons and beads for two or three hours. Some of the smaller buttons fit inside some of the larger ones, and quite a few of the beads are sparkly. It's just not something he can miss. He cannot, he regrets, even *stop by for a minute to say hi* because he needs to go the Big Y to buy $117 of groceries, even though his wife went shopping four days ago. He needs to leave in the car the snack he lovingly prepared so that his ravenous daughter, who is somehow never hungry at home, will have to eat food from the grocery store, which means that Abbott will end up purchasing an empty box and an empty bottle in the checkout line for $5.58. When, later, he puts away groceries, he'll just dump the box and bottle directly from the shopping bag into the recycling bin. He's going to be busy securing the string of the helium balloon from the bank branch inside the Big Y tightly around the handle of the shopping cart because his daughter will absolutely flip out if the balloon floats away. He hopes you understand. The invitation sounds great, and three or four years ago Abbott would have been the first to arrive and the last to depart, but regretfully, Abbott needs to hear from both the checker and the bagger at Big Y about how much milk he's buying. Three different kinds! While his daughter naps, Abbott will unfortunately still be occupied so he can't *sneak away* or *sneak anything in*. He promised his wife he would install a plastic locking device on the toilet-seat lid to prevent his daughter from dropping pennies in the bowl and laughing. Moreover, the veterinarian needs a urine sample from the dog and, if Abbott is reading his wife's note correctly, the cat. Regretfully, Abbott must also, throughout the day, construct and then dismantle the grandiose conviction that he is unappreciated, and this cycle of self-pity and self-reproach tends to be arduous and time-intensive. Abbott realizes the event could go on for quite awhile and be fun, but he's afraid he won't even be able to *swing by later* because the afternoon and evening are completely booked. He needs to go outside to play with pinecones, which always ends up taking way longer than you anticipate. Then it will be time to go inside to get some maple syrup rubbed into his hair, at which point he'll be busy clenching his jaw and reminding himself over and over that stewardship is a privilege, that he lives an enviable life, that by any important measure he is a profoundly fortunate man. Abbott knows, regretfully, that he also declined the last four invitations, and that at some point you're going to stop inviting him, but this day has been scheduled for a long time and there's nothing he can do to change it. Before you know it, it will be bath time, and he needs to be there to squirt the plastic raccoon. After the bath, he'll be going downstairs to pretend to look for something. If there is any time remaining in the day, which is unlikely, Abbott knows he should stop collecting acute and contradictory feelings for his wife, and spend just sixty seconds trying to imagine what it's like to be her. Now that he rereads the invitation, Abbott sees that the event to which he has been invited took place last weekend. It is with sincere regret that he sends this regretful note so late. He hopes you had a great time, and he reminds you that he would love to get together in four or five years for a coffee or maybe a beer.

24 Abbott Goes In

That crinkle Abbott hears as he undresses before bed is caused by the nu-merous plastic sleeves of juice-box straws stuffed into the pockets of the shorts he has worn for three days straight. Eventually he might ruminate about fluorocarbons and landfills, the domestication of the modern man, preschool dentistry, the lunatic conjunction of *juice* and *box*, but first he needs to sneak into his daughter's dark room. She lies on her back, way up on her pillow. The top of her head is pressed against the wall, and her face is turned severely to the side, away from Abbott. Her hands are fists at her throat. She is braced against sleep, as if against wind, a wave. Abbott's eyes adjust, but Abbott does not.

25 Abbott and the Antique Tractor

Sure, they could drive across the neighborhood, but it's more fun to walk. It's good exercise, and it's also nice to be outside in the summertime. Abbott dresses his daughter and gets her ready to leave. "OK, here we go," he says, opening the front door. He feels nearly euphoric. That noise in the front yard is the squirrels. "Let's go see the tractor," he says. A neighbor told him there's an antique tractor parked in the field directly behind the neighborhood, and he thought his daughter might want to see it. His wife, too. All of them. Here comes Abbott's wife with that belly. Abbott looks at her and feels the stirring of ancient, mutually exclusive impulses. His wife regards the girl's outfit. It's probably right what she's probably thinking. She says, "I don't really . . . For one thing, I have never even seen those pants." Abbott shrugs and says, "She picked them out." This isn't true. "Ready?" he says. "Let's get going. Tractor!" "Wait," his wife says. "Did you put sunblock on her?" Abbott nods his head in the manner of someone who could later deny having nodded. His wife looks right at him and says, "You did?" Abbott almost imperceptibly shakes his head. His wife says, "So you didn't?" Abbott nods again. His wife says, "Could you put some sunblock on her?" The girl says, "Tractor." Abbott closes the door. His wife says, "Does she have a new diaper?" Abbott's eyes become glassy and unfocused. He breathes audibly from his mouth. He feels unhappy and old and sleepy. "And I am sorry," his wife says, "but these are not summer pants. See, they have a *lining*." Abbott attempts to say that the girl chose the pants, but he's too tired to repeat the entire lie, and he falls silent. "She's already sweating," his wife says. "I'm not trying to be a bitch," she adds. Abbott tells his daughter they have to return to her room, and the child erupts. Tears actually seem to shoot forth from her face, as from the faces of animated characters. He picks her up and carries her through the house, knowing these days will soon seem, in comparison, like the easy days of a carefree summer. The girl keeps kicking him in the abdomen. Much later, prepared for the family outing, they walk back through the house together. Abbott's wife has packed some snacks and drinks. "OK, let's go see that tractor," she says, opening the door, accepting the tremendous burden of enthusiasm. Outside it is humid and resplendent. In the driveway there are, it turns out, two feathers, a berry, several chunks of tar, and a *lot* of pebbles. The girl begins to collect the items, and Abbott carries what she cannot hold in her hands, which is almost everything. Overhead, planes cross the sky, and Abbott's daughter stops to watch every one. "Plane," she says, pointing. "Plane." "Check out this weird bug," Abbott's wife says, pointing to something in the grass. The family checks out the weird bug. Neighborhood children ride by on their bicycles, captivating Abbott's daughter. Her naptime is looming. The tractor is an impossible dream. Nobody in Abbott's family will see an antique tractor today, if ever. Abbott's wife seems to have accepted this fact with grace and maturity. It occurs to Abbott that she may have known it all along. Abbott and his family have still not left the premises. "Who else is hungry?" Abbott's wife says. She sits on the blacktop and opens the bag of snacks. Abbott's daughter yelps and runs across the driveway to her mother. The way she runs. Abbott watches, trying to memorize it.

26 Abbott and the Families of Trapped Miners

Despite Henry David Thoreau's admonition that "If we read of one man robbed, or murdered, or killed by accident, or one house burned, or one vessel wrecked, or one steamboat blown up, or one cow run over on the Western Railroad, or one mad dog killed, or one lot of grasshoppers in the winter,—we never need read of another," Abbott nevertheless clicks tonight on an interview with the families of trapped miners. What he learns is that these families of trapped miners, like the families of trapped miners throughout the devastating history of mining, are tired and sad and recklessly hopeful. One woman whose husband is trapped holds six-week-old twins. She says she woke in the night because she heard his voice.

27 The Labors of Abbott

Returning home from a spectacularly unsuccessful quest to buy a couch, Abbott stops with his wife and daughter in the parking lot of a strip mall of premium outlet stores in Northern Connecticut. He's not shopping, though. What he's doing is cleaning vomited raspberries out of his daughter's car seat with antibacterial moist wipes. He is reminded of the exceptionally strong mythical hero who had to clean out the dirty stables. He is trying not to be reminded of the exceptionally strong mythical hero who had to perform the same bad job over and over. The moist wipes are cool and pleasing, with a faintly stringent odor, redolent of bactericide. The considerable mound of red-tinted towels is striking, nearly pretty, on the black tar. He glances up once to see his daughter running across the searing lot wearing yellow socks and a sagging diaper, looking very much like a child whose parents do not file federal income taxes. Abbott's wife chases the girl listlessly, pregnantly, in the heat. In one hand she holds the ruined clothes, in the other the clean clothes. In her uterus she carries another uncivilized human child. She appears to have no hope of catching the girl, much less of clothing her. Like a mythical hero, Abbott returns his attention to the car seat, the numerous crevices of which are coated in sweet-smelling gastric compote. She really ate a lot of raspberries. He removes the seat from the car and discovers that it is dripping somewhere from its center. There are brown birds in the parking lot picking off pieces of discarded bagel and croissant, then flying back to a crevice behind the Liz Claiborne sign, where they live and raise their children. They appear to be uninterested in his liver. Time has more or less stopped. Abbott's sweat drips down into the vomit, and he arrives again in paradox. The following propositions are both true: (A) Abbott would not, given the opportunity, change one significant element of his life, but (B) Abbott *cannot stand* his life.

28 Abbott the Activist

It's late and still awfully hot when Abbott inadvertently discovers, on the Internet, a petition to prohibit the painting of hermit crab shells. The petition is beautiful, Abbott understands, precisely because it is futile. He suspects that he would not like to be in the same room with any of these 298 dissenters, but he loves them virtually and from afar. There is distant thunder, and Abbott can hear the clicking of the trembling dog's toenails on the wood floor. He does not want to know what time it is. The miracle child is asleep in her bed, clutching a stuffed pony. He signs the petition with the letters of his keyboard, perhaps augmenting his modest file at the Federal Bureau of Investigation. Then, galvanized still, he changes the light bulb in his desk lamp.

29 Abbott Takes the Garbage Out

It's not as if Abbott is never struck by the sublime grandeur of existence. It's not as if he is never moved by the simple fact of being alive on this magnificently unlikely planet. Just this evening it happens as he is taking out the garbage. He places the cans by the curb, and when he turns to walk back to his house, the hazy summer light through the spruce trees brings him to a stop in his driveway. When language too quickly catches up, perhaps five or six seconds after he is halted by the splendor, the word that comes to Abbott's mind is *gratitude*. He is grateful to be alive, grateful to be a witness to beauty. So far, so good. But then Abbott recalls, as he not infrequently does, Kevin Carter's Pulitzer Prize–winning photograph of the young Sudanese girl who has collapsed on her way to a feeding station. It appears that her head is too heavy to lift off the sand. In the background a vulture waits on the ground with what looks in the photograph like patience. It's not an intrusive thought if you summon it, if you keep it close. The image abrades him like a hair shirt. The inevitable substitution of his daughter for this Sudanese girl does not increase Abbott's gratitude; rather, it warps the gratitude into guilt and sorrow, which are, like gratitude, insufficient to the problem. Abbott looks away from the hazy summer light through the spruce trees to his house, a 1955 ranch with vinyl siding and a Cape roof. What kind of fool would cherish this? What kind of fool would not cherish this? Carter's suicide note said, among other things, "The pain of life overrides the joy to the point that joy does not exist." He was survived by a wife and young daughter, who suffered for his response to suffering. Is Abbott afflicted by a problem of psychology or a problem of philosophy? Are these discrete problems? Are these rhetorical questions? Back inside the house, Abbott, reaching irritably, wonders if he has a *responsibility* to enjoy his life, given the material conditions of his existence. Preoccupation with suffering does not alleviate suffering. Preoccupation with suffering actually causes suffering. Therefore, it is both practical and ethical to ignore suffering . . . Perhaps a minute after his euphoric epiphany about the grandeur of existence, Abbott is standing at the kitchen counter, picking at scraps from the dirty dinner plates, not honoring or being at all conscious of this food and how it arrived on his family's plates. He's not even conscious of putting food in his mouth or chewing or swallowing. He's certainly not hungry. You're not, he knows, supposed to eat while standing. Might Abbott be *obliged* to take some delight in his existence? Deprivation ceases to have meaning if we do not recognize and enjoy that which is deprived. This is either correct or incorrect. Determined to make a sincere attempt at delight, Abbott returns to the driveway. Fortunately, the sunlight is still hazy and still shining through the spruce. He stares at the light and the trees and exhorts himself: *There, now, look—enjoy.* He attempts to risk delight, as the poet instructs. Perhaps it is a risk; perhaps it takes courage. Abbott fails to achieve a powerful sense of gladness. After eight or ten seconds he thinks, I am not thinking of the Sudanese girl. The mowers make the evening hum. There's a high branch, he notices, leaning heavy on a power line.

30 Abbott and the Bowl-Shaped Field

If he weren't an untenured humanist at the flagship campus of a state university system, what would Abbott most like to be? He's thought about this question and now he has an answer: He'd like to be a field scientist with a useless research project. While he does make himself click on the headline about the man who threw his three young children off a bridge to get back at his wife, he also, it should be noted, permits himself to click on the headline about the husband-and-wife team that has studied fireflies for the past eighteen years. During this time they have amassed copious data on the life cycle and mating habits of several species of lightning bugs. It's not much of a surprise to learn that the males with the brightest and longest flashes have the most reproductive success. In some species, the females return a blink two seconds after the male's blink; in other species, the interval is four seconds. The research is wonderful because it is so unnecessary. All it does is create knowledge. Abbott loves science without application or consequence. It's no mystery why they aren't divorced, these scientists. Or why they haven't stabbed or poisoned each other. For eighteen summers they have been conducting research in the same place in Pennsylvania. They sit on a jutting rock and look down at the fireflies blinking in a large bowl-shaped field. No vivisection, no monkeys, no Pentagon grants. They just observe and record the data. The man says the first night of each summer they never do any science. They used to try, but they gave it up. He says all these years and it's still an amazing sight. His wife agrees. It's like the sky is turned upside down, she says.

July

1 Abbott Bumps His Head on the Glass Ceiling of the Capitalist Imagination

This morning Abbott is sitting on his back deck having coffee and reading the *newspaper* with Ted, Margot, Oliver, Vince, and Chester, who are all imaginary people. Not friends, exactly, because Abbott does not have the time or energy to maintain the friendships. Acquaintances, let's say. Abbott says, "OK, everyone, listen to this," and he begins to read aloud a very interesting imaginary article about two identity thieves, ages sixteen and seventeen, who hatched and executed a bold scheme whereby they obtained the credit card information of numerous wealthy Americans and then used the cards to make generous (but not exorbitant) donations to worthy charities (children, animals), consequently putting the prosperous cardholders in the awkward position of contesting the transactions and retracting desperately needed donations to heroic nonprofit organizations. Shame as a lever. And if these fraud victims did not contest the charges, then in essence no crimes had been committed, and the kids would go unprosecuted. Abbott considers this article a kind of moral-political-spiritual Rorschach test, and he stops reading after five paragraphs to elicit comments from his acquaintances. Margot is laughing. She has her head tilted back and her mouth open with her buck teeth pointed upward as if to take a big bite out of the sky. She is gorgeous and buzzing. She pats Abbott on the forearm and says, "You just made my day." Abbott has a gigantic crush on Margot. If he were not married to a real woman and if he didn't have dried applesauce on his neck and if Margot were not always off backpacking through terrifying countries, he thinks he might propose to her this instant. But then Ted with that ridiculous facial hair says that he just doesn't think that the end ever justifies the means. Abbott shares a meaningful look with Margot; he rolls his eyes, and she sticks out her big red tongue. Ted says that these two fellows—he actually says *fellows*— broke the law and must face the consequences. He provides a brain-numb-ing series of examples and hypothetical scenarios to illustrate means/ ends ethics. And while he is genuinely sympathetic to all Robin Hoods . . . that's when Vince interrupts to say that these naïve hackers have an undeveloped political consciousness. Margot says, "They're sophomores in high school, Vince." Vince says, "So?" Margot says, "Can't you just admit that it's kind of cool?" Vince swats her question away with a wave of his hand. He says that injustice is systemic. You can't just strike rich in-dividuals, he says. You have to strike institutions and systems. These kids' actions are meaningless in the context of the larger struggle. Ultimately, they have done nothing to alter the access to the means of production. This is Vince's answer to everything. He is right, of course, but Abbott still wishes he would shut up. The deck furniture is imaginary and it is *nice*. This lazy expanse of Sunday morning is definitely imaginary. Oliver exclaims, "String those kids up and televise it!" This represents his full intellectual response to the matter. Nobody knows why Oliver is even allowed to be here. Then it's quiet for a moment, and everyone turns toward Chester, the fatalist. Generally, Chester does not speak unless prodded. "So, Chess," Margot says, "what do you think?" Chester looks up from Sports, the only section of the paper he says still has the capacity to surprise. "It doesn't matter what I think," he says fatalistically. "Sure it does," Margot says. "Just keep reading the article," Chester says, returning his attention to Sports. Abbott finds his place at the sixth paragraph and resumes reading out loud. As it turns out, twenty-two of the twenty-four wealthy fraud victims contested and withdrew the unlawful donations. Charity officials, quoted on condition of anonymity, found it difficult to hide their disgust. After a two-month investigation, the FBI apprehended the teenaged perpetrators at a skate park a few blocks from their high school. There was, apparently, something wrong with their plan at the level of conception. They are still being held and interrogated by the FBI, and will likely face charges of larceny and fraud. Said one law enforcement spokesman, "These little wiseguys are in a whole heap of trouble."

2 Abbott and the Disturbing Images

The one-year-old child in the home video that Abbott shot but did not
want to watch tonight is doing some adorable things that Abbott and
his wife had forgotten, even though they believed when they saw those
things, only a year ago, they would never forget them. For instance, she
is putting a ceramic serving bowl on her head. Abbott and Abbott's wife
watch without smiling. Abbott is stunned, and he does not know what
his wife is. The family room, past and present, looks post-tornadic. That
child, so alive right now on the television, is missing, gone forever. That
ceramic serving bowl, a wedding present, has also disappeared. Abbott
does not want to pick a fight. He does not want to spoil the evening with
gloom. But how else to say it—mortality permeates home video. Those
tragic anti-drunk-driving television commercials from Abbott's youth—
the ones featuring home-video footage of joyous children subsequently
killed by drunk drivers—those ads did not create the association. They
presumed it, utilized it. Nevertheless, Abbott keeps his mouth shut.
"You're right," Abbott's wife says after only a few minutes of adorable footage. "You're right. Let's not." A child is a Trojan horse, *a thing of guile.* The
rout is commenced.

3 Abbott and the Terrible Persistence of Romantic Thought

Yesterday morning, compelled as if by some binding treaty or biological imperative or perhaps *The Farmer's Almanac*, many of the men in Abbott's neighborhood rose early to clean their gutters. Abbott, more vulnerable to this kind of suburban pressure than he'd care to admit, today borrows a ladder and climbs it roofward during the hottest part of the day. The rain gutter is an apt synecdoche of domestic existence: From the ground it appears practical, functional, well conceived. But when you stand on a borrowed ladder and peer into it, you realize what a gutter is. A gutter is a flimsy trough of sludge, secured by rusty hardware. Rainwater is not so much channeled and diverted as collected and absorbed. All along the front of his house Abbott is alternately repulsed and terrified. He is afraid of falling off the ladder and sustaining compound fracture or death. The warning is right there on the top step, accompanied by a picture of a tumbling man who also appears to be on fire. Abbott knows that one instant everything is OK and then the next instant everything is not. He knows that it's always the husbands of pregnant women who get buried by sinkholes or lashed by falling power lines. But he continues scooping the muck into a black garbage bag, and by the time he reaches the gutter along the back of his house, his dread and aversion have abated, and his eye and mind begin to wander. He sees that the roof over his family room runs flat until it hits the roof over his garage, where it rises at a soft angle for three feet or so before peaking and dropping steeply down the other side. Abbott, now accustomed to the ladder and his repetitive gutter-cleaning movements thereon, knows that there are two kinds of people in the world: those who would climb onto the flat roof one lovely summer night with a blanket and a bug-repelling candle and a bottle of cheap wine in order to recline against the gentle slope of the garage roof and gaze up at the vastness with a wine-bent conception of the sublime so limited as to be *soothing,* and those who would not. Of the latter type, Abbott knows that there are two subtypes: those who would not, beyond adolescence, even think to climb onto the roof with a frayed backpack one lovely summer evening, and those who would envision it deeply and repetitively, but never, ever do it. Abbott belongs to this wretched latter subtype, the worst possible. All that vestigial poetic yearning, useless and malignant. Abbott's wife, inside the house, comes to the kitchen window below the section of the gutter that Abbott is cleaning. Her face in the window is level with his thighs, and so naturally he imagines her sucking his penis and swallowing his semen. "Are they bad?" she asks. "The gutters?" "Yeah." "They're not that bad," he says, lying for no reason at all. She says, "The baby is really kicking today."

4 Abbott Celebrates the Birth of His Nation

Abbott knows what's going on out there. Blankets on lawns, scared birds circling the dark, the smell of burnt meat, sulfur. Somewhere a minivan in neutral is gliding silently toward the pond. Abbott is unpatriotic, unwashed. He pours another drink, kills a mosquito, sedates his dog with laced cheddar. He can hear, in the distance, the Sousa and bottle rockets. He reads *Billy Budd, Sailor* for the first time in seventeen years. He had forgotten how sad it is, or more likely he had never quite known.

5 In Which the Celebration Continues Deep into the Night

Poor welkin-eyed Billy, devoid of *sinister dexterity*. The days can be long without it, Abbott knows. He's lying in bed beside his wife, who is almost certainly awake. These two heads on pillows, maybe three feet apart. Budd's tragic impressment by the Royal Navy has Abbott remembering the day, nearly thirty years ago, when he learned about military conscription. His father had made some casual remark about his exemption from the draft, young Abbott had asked for a clarification of terms, and his parents, still married then, had explained. What a concept. What a blow to moral intuition. (This was roughly six months before the intuition-razing twelve-hour television miniseries *Roots*.) Abbott can recall the backyard patio, the dandelions, the squat tin shed flexing in the heat. He received his parents' warm but dubious assurance that he would never be conscripted and then went upstairs and closed his door. Thirty years ago in a backyard. Abbott, lying now in bed, has an idea. He might put his forehead right against hers if she'll turn around. The firecrackers still cracking out there, the sedated dog snoring at the foot of the bed. "Hey," he whispers, turning on his side to face his wife's shape.

6 The Heating and Cooling Specialist's Tale

"I come to this guy's house in the middle of the afternoon, and he's home. I figure he's probably a professor. I'm a little early, and he seems kind of startled to see me. He comes to the door holding his daughter." "How old is she?" "I don't know, I can't tell anymore. Two? The guy's arm is completely covered with butterfly stickers, and he's wearing all this costume jewelry. Like that kind Sarah used to love. Three or four bracelets and probably *ten* necklaces this guy's wearing. His daughter is just in a diaper, and she has magic-marker streaks all over her chest and legs. They're listening to Tom Petty's *Damn the Torpedoes*. You know, I've been there, those long days, no big deal, but this guy looks a little sheepish, even after I tell him I have a daughter and try to make funny faces at the girl and all that." "You scared her, didn't you?" "She just looked at me. Then the guy shows me into the kitchen, and I see his dog, this big Lab, jammed into a tiny space between the dishwasher and the cabinet, and the dog is trembling and drooling like crazy. Just like Otis used to do when it thundered, except today it was beautiful. And I think maybe he'll try to explain the dog, but he doesn't say anything. So I say, 'Your refrigerator isn't working?'

And he tells me that it's just not keeping the food very cold. I open it up, and I look in, and it's filled with juice and fake meat, so now I know the guy is a professor." "You look at people's food?" "Hey, I don't judge. And the first thing I always check when there's a problem with a fridge—just in case—is the little temperature dial. You know? Like you turn it one way to make it—" "I know what the dial is." "And sure enough, I move this huge thing of apple juice and about three gallons of milk to look at the dial, and it's turned all the way to the warmest setting. So that's the problem with the fridge. That's why he called me out there." "Oh, God." "I know." "I think even I would know to check that dial." "And I know this guy is going to be humiliated about this, so I'm trying to explain the problem while still facing into the refrigerator, and I'm moving very slowly and trying to make it seem like it's requiring some expertise to, you know, turn the dial to a higher number. And I tell him that's the first thing he should always check when there's a problem." "Were you an ass about it?" "No, not at all. I was serious and professional. This could happen to anyone, and that's what I told him. I told him I see it every day, which believe me I don't. And when I finally close the door and turn around, the guy is kind of smiling, but he won't make eye contact." "That's horrible." "I am taking no pleasure in any of this. And he's still holding his daughter, and she's patting his head and saying, 'Good boy, Dad,' over and over. Then we just stand there in the kitchen, and it's awkward. The only noise is the dog, who is trembling so hard in that little nook or whatever that you can *hear* it. And then I have to tell him it's forty dollars for the visit. It's supposed to be sixty—and Ray will give me shit about it—but I just can't do it to this guy." "You're sweet. You are." "And he says sure, sure, and he writes me a check while holding his daughter, and she's sticking a dinosaur into his ear and saying, 'Dino in Dad's ear.' And then he hands me the check, and things are still kind of awkward, so I point at Sarah outside in the van in the driveway and tell him I've got my girl with me today. And I tell him she's sixteen and we're on our way to go upgrade her cell phone. And we both look out the window at her—she's got her feet up on the dash, and she's painting her toenails." "No, she wasn't." "Yes, she was too. And she had that bored-looking kind of scowl on her face." "I know the one." "And honey, I have no idea why I'm talking so much to this guy. I just want to leave. This is more than I usually say in a week on the job. But then for some reason I tell him what I promised myself I would never say to anyone because I got so sick of hearing it when Sarah was little, but I said it." "I don't believe it." "Yes, I did. I said, 'Man, enjoy it now because it just goes by *so fast*.'" "Wow." "And now I'm mortified, too, and the situation has gotten unbearable. The dog I swear seems like his heart might explode." "What did he say?" "He didn't say anything. He kind of laughed, and then I laughed too. Then he shook my hand and took the girl back into the playroom before I even put away the paperwork and got my tools. When I left, he was down on the floor, throwing her way up in the air and catching her."

7 In Which Abbott Is Linked to Fetal Research in New Zealand

Because of the weak dial-up connection tonight, the Internet video of the stranger's sonogram loads slowly and plays haltingly. The image is grainy and blurry. Nevertheless, after viewing the clip six or seven times, Abbott can pretty clearly see that the fetus is sobbing. The narrator, a professor at the University of Auckland, explains that the unborn child, twenty-eight weeks old, is responding to a vibro-acoustic stimulus (or a loud noise, if Abbott understands correctly). The narrator, nine thousand miles from Abbott, points out the rapid phases of inspiration and expiration, the three augmented breaths, the heaving chest, the tilt of the head. When a fetus cries like this, researchers call it fetal crying. Two hundred days, roughly speaking. "Wait," Abbott's wife says later, "it can cry before it can breathe?" Abbott lies completely still. He has never been so vibro-acoustically cautious. "Even the chin quivers," he says.

8 Abbott Recoils from the Natural Order of Things

Abbott means no harm. His daughter is frightened of spiders, even the kind called daddy longlegs, and Abbott is attempting to relocate the spider by gently grasping one of its legs. His daughter is weeping and running in circles, and so perhaps he rushes the job. The leg comes off. These things are as thin as hairs. He is not at all surprised when the seven-legged spider makes a swift escape through the grass. He is surprised, however, when its recently severed leg *also* escapes, twitching nimbly across the bright yellow ledge of his daughter's inflatable pool. One must not be rash in ascribing human attributes to a detached spider leg, but the leg does seem to move with determination, courage, and a complete lack of self-pity. And later this day, Abbott, driving home from the Big Y out on Route 9, passes a construction site where an out-and-out *meadow* of two-foot weeds grows on the steep slope of a mound of truck-dumped dirt. The weeds sway and bend for the sun just like real plants. This bogus hillock will no doubt be dozed anon; the grading vehicles are parked on-site, ready. Nevertheless, the weeds just keep photosynthesizing. Their seeds are dispersed carelessly, ingeniously, in the summer breeze. This is the Holy Land, apparently. They all grow another sixteenth of an inch as Abbott drives past. "*Enough*," he yells at the construction-site weeds. His daughter sits in the backseat with her pronouns all mixed up. "You want some songs," she says. "You want a peanut. You want."

9 Abbott Glimpses, As If from a Distance

Mornings, Abbott often finds the evidence of his wife's sleeplessness: a used tea bag in a mug, a wrinkled pillow, a novel tossed on the couch. And of course her occasional notes, written on scraps of ripped paper and left by the coffeemaker. Months ago, when they began appearing, the notes were darkly comic, apologetic, tender. They digressed into observation and affection before requesting that Abbott please allow her to sleep in the morning. Often they included the time. The ripped scraps of paper were larger then, and the entreaties frequently ran to the back side of the paper. The notes have steadily gotten shorter, the scraps smaller. Abbott's wife has now nearly abandoned rhetorical flourish, arrangement, punctuation, penmanship, and the small rightward arrow that signifies continuation. *Long night—sorry.* Or, the last time, simply: *3:30 bad.* Abbott has saved all these notes in a manila folder without knowing why. There are three digital clocks in the kitchen—one on the microwave, one on the stove, one on the coffeemaker. They must be awful in the night. The insomniac cannot even take comfort in their small discrepancies because Abbott synchronizes them after each electrical outage. They are unanimous, imperious. This morning he sees, as he enters the kitchen, the aggressive display of time, as well as that tiny shard of white paper by the coffeemaker. Though he is morbidly curious about the note, he does not by now need to read it to know what it means. His wife must know this too, because the note, Abbott comes to learn, does not have a word on it.

10 The Broken Heart It Kens

In the basement Abbott presses shirts he will not have occasion to wear for three to four months. Each one has an ink stain, the insignia of his guild. This last wrinkled shirt is gray with two black dots on the shoulder. Abbott has moved into the final stage of ironing, during which he attempts to iron out the wrinkles that he previously ironed in. The monitor hisses quietly on the ironing board, Abbott's daughter having long ago stopped singing a Scottish folk song about a captured Jacobite Highlander who will never again see his true love on the banks of a beautiful lake, and whose soul, after his body is executed by English soldiers, will travel through the spirit world, arriving home in Scotland well before his extant rebel comrade, who will walk home alone over the Earth. The static of the monitor and the sibilant chugs of the iron, combined with the dim light of a dust-covered, low-watt bulb and the stale subterranean air and the metal shelves full of rusty cans of paint and turpentine, make Abbott feel as if he is the sole survivor of a calamitous event in some remote expeditionary outpost. His shirts are beautiful, though, like Gatsby's. They remind him of the purpose of art. He unplugs the iron and pockets the monitor. He picks up the neat warm rectangular bundle of stained shirts, turns off the light, and begins to climb the stairs in darkness. Somewhere between the bottom of the stairs and the top, he strikes his knee against a metal bracket that connects the railing to the wall. He falls to a sitting position, grips his knee with both hands. His pressed shirts tumble down the dark stairs. The pain is immense, and it does not abate. Rather, it escalates, takes on new dimensions and nuances, opens into meaninglessness. The pain lacks value and context. If Abbott's wife were here, she would turn on the light and say, "Oh, God, ouch. What did you *do*?" She would offer him the ice that he would refuse for no conceivable reason. She would say, "Here, let me see it." She would look at the knee and, no matter what she saw, she would grimace. The pain would stand for something; it would exist in a sense *for* his wife, for the marriage. It would conceivably lead to some kind of physical intimacy, perhaps right here on the stairs. Abbott and his wife might explore the erotic potential of a serious knee injury. But she's not here and he can't call for her. Or he won't. This pain—his shoulders are shaking, his teeth chattering, as if he has been pulled from an icy pond. Abbott cannot determine if he is nearer the top or the bottom. Ascension, though, is out the question, so he scoots painfully down, over the pile of his ironed shirts. Streetlight enters the room through the small ground-level windows at the top of the basement walls, and the pupils of Abbott's eyes automatically dilate so that he can make out shapes and edges in the dark. He hops on his noninjured leg toward his bourgeois cache of unused furniture. He sees a plastic-wrapped crib mattress leaning against a rocking chair, and he topples it to the ground. Abbott lies down on the tiny mattress, his legs extending far off the edge. The plastic covering crinkles beneath him as he adjusts his body. The smell of mildew makes him feel as if he himself is rotting. He has seen images of spores, magnified many times. When his breathing finally slows, the basement becomes quiet and he can hear the hum of the fan in his bedroom, directly above. He can hear his wife turning in bed. For a few minutes he considers masturbation. A passing car's headlights briefly illuminate the room, and Abbott sees an old flashlight on an old bedside table, within reach. He picks it up and turns it on. Its light is weak and yellow. First he sits up and shines the light on his knee, which is still vibrating with pain. He fears and expects to see something commensurate with the sensation—chips of bone under skin or a lurid contusion or grotesque swelling—but his fear turns to disappointment when he notices that there is not a mark on it. His knee just looks like the knee of a guy in his late thirties. Next he shines the light on the stairs. The shirts are strewn, as if they had grappled at the top and then tumbled down. Their backs look broken. A blue one has an arm outstretched, as if trying to break its fall, or to reach for something out of reach.

11 Abbott and the Clenched Jaw

At whom can Abbott be angry? "Another amazing Friday night," he says to his wife as they clip the dog's toenails in the foyer. Abbott's dog lies compliantly on the tile floor, but his eyes are wild with terror and his limbs are trembling. "It's OK," Abbott's wife says to the dog. "This won't hurt. You're doing great." Abbott's knee hurts. He is angry with the dog, though he understands it is unfair to blame the dog for everything. He notices for the first time that there seems to be some kind of rot in the grout between the tiles. "We should brush his teeth, too," Abbott's wife says. "Look at that brown stuff." "It's always such a relief when the weekend comes," Abbott says. "Don't cut them too short," says his wife. "It's a chance to kick back and blow off some steam," he says. With a little pep and tonal diligence, these words might possibly convey a tenderly ironic statement of solidarity, rather than a jagged statement of anger poorly disguised as a tenderly ironic statement of solidarity. "One more foot, buddy," Abbott's wife says. "You're doing great." "This is why we work so hard," Abbott says. "It's all worth it when the weekend comes." Abbott's dog makes a halfhearted attempt at escape, and Abbott pushes him back down to the floor. "Just relax!" he shouts at the dog. "First of all?" Abbott's wife says. "This is not Friday." Abbott says, "Fine." She says, "It's not even close to Friday." Abbott says, "The point still holds." "What point is that?" his wife asks. Abbott is not quite sure he knows what his point is. He has a notion, but it's too terrible to say out loud. He pets the dog, examines a paw. "Second, it's not my fault and it's not his fault," Abbott's wife says, "so don't take it out on us." She kneels on the tile by the dog, scratching his ear. Abbott has been trying, he realizes, to look down her shirt. "Fine," he says. "I know." "And third?" she says, "do you even remember how hard I had to try to get you to go out on a Friday night before we had a kid?" Abbott says, "That's not true," which is not true. Meanwhile, the developing fetus can hear this whole pitiful encounter, according to the Internet. You would think the amniotic fluid would muffle sound, but it actually amplifies it. For an analogy, it might be helpful to remember how well you could hear underwater in the county swimming pool of so long ago.

12 Abbott Discovers an Idiom in His Yard

Abbott's neighbor's woodpile, against which Abbott pushes his mower this afternoon, is a real woodpile, not a metaphor. Abbott, deep in academic reverie, doesn't even recognize the object, doesn't name it *woodpile.* It's been reduced to its geometry—it exists only in relation to his mower. As he bumps the mower against the edge of the pile, he is startled by an interstitial slithering in the stacked logs. He sees the scales, so vivid as to seem artificial. Numerous times in his professional life, in hallways and department meetings, Abbott has heard the phrase *snake in the woodpile.* It's a stock expression of the paranoid intellectual. *I know about snakes in woodpiles,* Abbott thinks, sprinting across his yard away from the snake in the woodpile, *but what is that snake doing in that woodpile?* This is what it's like living life backwards. He can't catch his breath. Once again he's stunned by the real.

13 Abbott Thinks, Yet Again, the Unthinkable

Abbott's daughter has been napping for two hours and fifty minutes. Abbott, a frequent complainer about her short naps, thinks this one has been going on entirely too long. The monitor is quiet, which means either that she is alive and sleeping or that she is no longer alive. He wishes he had been more patient with her, more attentive. He wishes he had been more focused and engaged during all those hours they spent with the beads and the buttons in the family room. He wonders about the last thing he said to her. He thinks it was, "Have a good one." When he has wrestled and played with her in the family room, he has put his head on her chest and heard her small heart beating. He has wondered what keeps it going and going. Nobody seems willing to admit that the very premise is outlandish. Abbott's daughter's nap is Abbott's time to get things done around the house or run errands or rest or read, but for the past forty-five minutes he has just been sitting at the dining-room table, waiting for her to wake up. There is no good reason to go in to check on her. If her heart is not beating, *then it has already stopped beating.* Going in does not change that. Why enter her room only to confirm a dark suspicion? While there exists the possibility that she is alive and napping, Abbott should remain outside her room. If the nap lasts five hours, a week, a month, he should sit right here at the dining-room table with the slim hope that she's just very tired. Why not live as much of his life as possible with this hope? Why rush to begin the sorrowful remainder of his days? If she is no longer alive, every second he does not know for certain that she is no longer alive is another second he does not have to live with it. He knows it is best to stay out of her room. When he enters her room, she immediately stirs. She is, and has been, alive. His relief is immediately succeeded by regret and self-rebuke. He does not want her to wake up. He could be reading right now, or taking his own nap. He could be working with wood. He tries to sneak from the room, but his daughter sits up and calls out. "Dad," she says, rubbing her eyes. "Dad. I'm awake."

14 Abbott's Imaginary Burst into Subdisciplinary Prominence

"Historically speaking," Abbott begins before a rapt imaginary audience at the imaginary Royal Institute of Harbinger, Omen, and Portent in Helsinki, "we occupy the epoch after Juvenal and before Armageddon." He pauses for robust laughter, as his notes instruct. His imaginary paper is called "On the Feasibility of American Burlesque." Its real thesis is that it's increasingly unfeasible. The ornate, high-ceilinged lecture hall is stiflingly hot or quite drafty and cold. The atmosphere is electric, charged, and crackling. His artful Power Point presentation culminates with a photograph of the four deceased dolphins that recently washed up in San Diego. "A necropsy confirmed that they had been shot," Abbott says. "With a gun." The applause lasts one minute and thirty-five seconds. Flash photographers flout the strict prohibition against flash photography. Abbott's handkerchief is soaked. He looks up from the lectern, sees members of the audience scanning the conference program for his short and humble bio. It hasn't been easy to be away from his real wife and daughter for these six imaginary days, but the benefit to his career is inestimable.

His absence makes him miss and appreciate his family even more. This trip in all likelihood has strengthened the domestic bonds. Also, he has never been to Sweden, and he has enjoyed discovering a new place on his own. Finland, he means. He has never been to Finland, and he has enjoyed discovering a new place on his own.

15 On the Very Possibility of Kindness

The bananas in the kitchen are overripe, and Abbott's wife wants to make banana bread. So far the premise is simple and so is the motivation. But there is a complication. Abbott's wife is tired and busy, and she is having trouble finding the time to make the bread. Right now she has to leave the house to get some milk and swimming diapers. After Abbott puts his daughter to bed for her nap, he walks into the kitchen and sees on the counter the perfectly overripe bananas, the large mixing bowl, and the recipe. What happens next is that he begins to make the banana bread, despite the fact that he has never baked anything. One can't presume to know another's thoughts, but Abbott feels certain that his wife did not leave the bananas, bowl, and recipe on the counter so that he might make the bread. He knows it would never occur to her that he would make the bread. Abbott is not even considering this possibility—it's just that when he sees these items on the counter he feels no twinge of guilt or responsibility, no subtle marital pressure, no implicit request or demand. He knows—to the extent this knowledge is possible—that his wife began to make the bread, but then ran out of time or energy. He knows she is not now at the Big Y wondering if her husband fell into the trap she set in the kitchen. He has already begun assembling ingredients when he notices that his wife has made notes on the recipe card, adjusting the amounts of ingredients to make a two-banana loaf rather than a three-banana loaf. He thinks with fondness of his wife, who keeps these adjusted recipe cards somewhere in their home. He doesn't really think; he just feels fondness. Fondness and a kind of jolt. He follows the adjusted recipe. His motivations for baking are unclear, even to himself. He's just baking, and at some point in the process he realizes he is enjoying himself, a realization that leads to an overawareness of baking and the enjoyment of baking, which threatens to spoil the experience but does not. He puts the loaf in the oven and waits. As the kitchen begins to smell good, he becomes eager for his wife's return. He is anxious to witness her surprise. He is anxious, he supposes, to be regarded as a surprising husband. Abbott is beginning to understand that he baked only because he believed his wife had absolutely no expectation that he would bake. Consequently, in making banana bread he could also make himself, at least temporarily, into a remarkable spouse. He may have thought he was helping his life partner, but he was not. Not in an authentic way. He was never baking *for her.* Now he has gone and spoiled the experience, and when she comes home he is gloomy with the certainty that he has never been and will never be genuinely *nice,* a quality he admires. He wishes he had not baked the bread. That would have been the nice thing to do. He walks out into the rain to help bring in the groceries, but not in a nice way. "What's wrong with you?" she asks, to which he just shakes his head. When she enters the house and smells the bread baking, she seems legitimately confused. It's as if—Abbott is just guessing here—it's as if she can't remember whether or not she made this bread. She can't remember making it, and yet the bread is obviously baking, so she searches her mind for other possibilities, finally arriving at her husband. "Did you make the banana bread?" she asks. "Yes," he says, unpacking groceries. "Are you serious?" she says. She opens the oven door and peeks in at the loaf, which is rising beautifully. Then, concerned, she says, "Did you follow the recipe for two bananas?" "Yes," he says. "Did you find the baking soda?" "Yes," he blurts, as if offended. She clearly cannot believe he found the baking soda. He himself had been stunned to find it earlier in the door of the refrigerator. "Well," Abbott's wife says, "thank you. That was nice." Together they put away the groceries in silence. Eventually he says, "I thought you might be surprised." "I *am*," she says. "I am surprised. And I'm grateful. I honestly can't believe you found the baking soda." This is not going well; the quality and quantity of her surprise are wrong. The afternoon has arrived at a shameful crisis: Even though Abbott knows that baking bread in order to exhibit his limitless depth is solipsistic and spiritually deficient—the very opposite of generous, in fact, and the cause of his current despondency—yes, even though he knows it, *he still wants his wife to notice his limitless depth.* "I was just trying to help you out," he says, casting a wide net across the True/False Continuum. "Listen," Abbott's wife says, squeezing the back of Abbott's neck, "the bread is a surprise, but you are not." And so it is that Abbott is surprised.

16 Abbott and the Mail

Fucking Thoreau—he could, for his part, *happily do without the post-office.*
Leave it to the childless to be complacent about the mail. You put a toddler in Walden and you'd get new philosophy. For *his* part, Abbott takes
great comfort in the reliable work of the postal service, a representative of
which comes to his neighborhood in the mid- to late afternoon six days a
week, every week. The mail is an undeniably significant part of his day. It
not only signals the blessed arrival of the mid- to late afternoon, it also offers the promise of surprise and wonder. Today there is nothing surprising
or wonderful, and in fact there never is. But there is the promise. Today
it's a bill and three more baby catalogues. Abbott and his wife used to feel
irked and mildly infringed upon by the fact that these companies somehow knew they were going to have a baby. But then they started flipping
through the catalogues, and they found a lot of interesting stuff. Abbott
sees four neighbors from four houses on his side of the street, all walking
to or from their mailboxes. The mail truck is still moving down the street,
and it continues to draw more neighbors from their houses. The scene
feels a bit like a nature documentary. Everyone greets one another in a

mechanical fashion, waving first to their eastern neighbors and then to their western neighbors. It's like they're all riding in a parade. Abbott does not even focus his eyes on a person or people—he just transmits vague signals of salutation to his counterparts. This is, to the best of Abbott's knowledge, a weekday. Don't his neighbors have jobs? And what could they all be expecting every day that is so important? Why this desperate rush? The awkward trip to the mailbox is enough to make Abbott want to wait a few minutes each day after delivery before checking his mail. On the other hand, he knows there are limits to what a man can ask of himself.

17 Abbott Adds a Key to the Ring

Abbott does not consider the broken doorknob on the seldom-used front door a high-priority repair, or even a problem. "So we can't get out," he says to his wife. "People can't get in. It's kind of a nice feature." "But what if there was a fire?" his wife says. She is a very skilled wife. This afternoon, during the child's nap, Abbott drives to the hardware store to purchase a doorknob. He stands in the doorknob aisle for fifteen minutes. Faced with a choice between many seemingly identical doorknobs, Abbott purchases the second most expensive one and takes it home in a bag. The installation is supposed to be easy, but it is not. The doorknob and the screwdriver become slippery in the moist air. The dropped screws clatter and vanish. Eventually, Abbott replaces the doorknob, then makes small noises and gestures of completion until his wife says, "Looks good. Nice job." Since Abbott did not replace the deadbolt, which was not broken, he now has two different keys for a door he does not use. He puts the new key on his ring, which has become heavy and crowded. What is that blue one for? It was only seven years ago—no, six—that Abbott left Texas in a small moving truck, after completing his lease and donating his Plymouth Reliant to an organization that teaches troubled teens to fix transmissions. At that point he had no keys. Not one. A putative adult with an empty key ring. He had forsaken the air-conditioning on his drive out of Texas. He had opened the windows and let the hot wind blow freely through the cab. The last time he told this story to his wife, she laughed and said, "Why don't you just tell me about a woman you enjoyed having sex with?" Stepping onto his porch with his screwdriver and jangling keys, he recalls the story of the empty key ring with a powerful sense of boredom. He closes the front door and tests the new doorknob and the lock. He turns and pushes, turns and pulls. He listens for the click, and he hears it.

18 Abbott on the Couch

Tonight Abbott is a generality, a tendency, a convention. He is an indistinct and featureless lump beneath a thin blanket. Tonight he is Husband on Couch. The battered cushions sag beneath the weight of his unoriginality. He is complicit, he knows. Nobody can make you be Husband on Couch. Wife in Big Bed can't. You always have choices. Abbott could hop a freight train, ride the rails, build fires in trash cans. Or he could be Husband on Air Mattress, just for the principle. The fight was painfully stupid. Abbott, lying in bed, asked his wife if her novel is any good. She said, "Oh, you know." Then he asked what her novel is about. He didn't even care; he was just making bedtime conversation. She said, "Oh, you know." He studied the title, the cover. He tried to peek at the author photograph. He said, "I do know. It's about marriage and secrets and faith. Am I right? And the strange settling sounds an old house makes at night? And that angle of light in the winter?" Abbott's wife did not say anything. Abbott said, "Loss of youth. Estrangement. A nice meal ruined by the truth. A long walk during which it becomes shockingly evident that the natural world is violent and ruthless." Abbott's wife said, "Are you done?" Abbott said, "*Passion*. Memory. Forgiveness. Seething things beneath a placid surface. A tree cleft by lightning." Abbott's wife closed her book and said, "Is there something you'd like to talk about?" Abbott realized that he was spoiling any chance of a good night's sleep for his wife, but he knew if he stopped now it would appear that he knew he was acting poorly, and that was not an admission he was prepared to make. He was operating by a strongly felt but dimly understood sense of correctness. "The smell of the cut grass, the feel of the cut grass on bare feet, the memories of walking on cut grass with bare feet in simpler times." Abbott's wife said, "Stop yelling." Abbott said, "I'm not." Abbott's wife said, "If there's something you'd like to say to me, then say it." Abbott said, "She lives in upstate New York with her husband, her two children, and her two horses." Abbott's wife said she didn't care about the novel but he was being an ass. And of course she rolled over to face away from him. It had taken Abbott, without premeditation, something like two minutes to wreck the night. Then, apropos of nothing beyond his own insensitivity, he said, "I know about the water in the basement." He found a tone to make it cruel. He got out of bed and stood up. Abbott's wife held her book with her index finger marking her place. She did not move and did not speak. Beside her, on her nightstand, that small porcelain dish filled with earplugs. He left the room and arrived unimaginatively on the horrible family-room couch, a stained and cat-tattered mound of soft dough. The dog came with him, but then returned to the bedroom after a few minutes. Abbott does not anticipate falling asleep anytime soon, but the next thing he knows his wife is shaking his leg. He opens his eyes to see her holding her novel and a steaming mug. The lamplight makes him squint. He rubs his eyes, pats the listless cushions for her to lie down with him. "This is my spot," she says. Abbott extracts himself from the couch and limps down the hallway, dragging his thin blanket like a vagabond. That's way too fast, he thinks, hearing a car drive past his house.

19 Abbott and the Sticky Shit All Over the Fucking Steering Wheel Again

Gone are the daydreams of academic notoriety and glistening vulvas and whatever else. All Abbott wants right now—the only thing—is to be knocked unconscious by the long wooden handle of a lawn tool.

20 Abbott and the Utopian Community

With his helpmeet Abbott establishes one early-summer evening a small utopian community in a seventh-floor room of a Boston-area La Quinta. After checking into the hotel, Abbott and his wife and daughter ride the elevator to the seventh floor, stopping at the second, fifth, and sixth floors because Abbott let his daughter push the buttons. Inside the room, Abbott says, "This is OK," and his wife says, "Yeah, it's fine." While Abbott holds the child on the window ledge overlooking heavy highway traffic ("Truck! Bus!"), his wife spreads out a picnic dinner on the comforter of the king-sized bed. There are peanut butter and honey sandwiches, sliced carrots and cucumbers, a sandwich bag of Fig Newtons, one ripe banana, and a large bottle of a sports energy drink that they all pass around and dribble onto the comforter. After dinner, Abbott puts a rusty barrette in his daughter's hair and the family rides down the elevator, walks out of the lobby, and discovers a tiny plot of grass by the parking lot. Nearly all of this utopian grass has been killed, either by dog urine or grubs. A high chain-link fence separates the play area from the busy highway. Abbott runs wildly in small circles, and his daughter chases him, stopping occasionally to put Styrofoam cups and blades of dead grass on a fire hydrant. Abbott's wife is too pregnant to run, but she watches and cheers and exclaims. Then they all return to the elevator and ride back up to the seventh-floor room. Abbott and his wife work together to put their daughter in pajamas, to brush her miniature teeth and wash her face. They turn out the lights, close the curtains to block the glow of the setting sun, and place the girl, along with her stuffed pony, in a playpen/crib in the corner. "Goodnight, sweetie," they say, moving a large utopian chair in front of the playpen/crib. "Have good dreams." But the child gets teary and is obviously not going to sleep, so Abbott moves the large chair and lies down on the floor next to the playpen/crib, the vinyl mesh siding of which allows him to speak to his daughter and to see her in the dim light. She rolls to the edge of the playpen/crib with her stuffed pony and says, "Dad's down." She says, "Dad's on the floor. There's Dad. See Dad through the hole. Hi, Dad. Dad has two knees. Airplane far away." Abbott says, "It's time to go to sleep." His daughter says, "Dad through the hole. Sunblock tastes bad. Toast is food. This is Popo. Show Popo to Dad? Hi, Popo. Mama's driving. This is a different blue one. We saw lions!" She begins singing the alphabet song, veers into "Twinkle, Twinkle, Little Star," then returns triumphantly to her version of the alphabet. "Good night," Abbott says, rising to his knees after fifteen or twenty minutes. His daughter says, "Dad? Dad, lie down! OK? That's fine. Dad through the hole!" So Abbott lies back down on the floor and talks to his daughter through the vinyl mesh of the playpen/crib. He feels as if he is either giving or receiving confession. His daughter says, "Dad's tired. Dad's rough. OK!" Once more he tries to get up and once more he is ordered to stay. The despot behind the mesh weighs less than a bag of dog food. Seventy minutes after being placed down, Abbott's daughter falls asleep, and Abbott creeps away from her, silently replacing the large chair in front of the playpen/crib. He finds his wife sitting cross-legged on the floor in the closet-and-sink niche outside the bathroom. The light from the bathroom is just enough for her to read a celebrity and fashion magazine. Abbott sits beside her, and they share a Hershey bar and look at dresses and purses and DWI mug shots. They're both too tired to be sardonic. Later, in the king-sized bed, Abbott wants to attempt late-term utopian intercourse, but his wife does not, so they compromise on a hand job. This is just fine with Abbott. He understands that compromise is a vital component of marriage, as is, though to a lesser extent, the hand job. In fact, as he approaches orgasm—or more likely, much later—he realizes that the hand-job-within-marriage, while no substitute for vow-renewing egalitarian coitus (from each according to his abilities, to each according to his needs), nevertheless does have a legitimate place in the utopian scheme. He rubs his wife's swollen belly as she does it. Afterward, she brings him a washcloth. They kiss goodnight, then roll to distant regions of the enormous bed. The next day is a disaster. The amazing furniture clearance is not amazing. There are too many other people and too many other people's children. Abbott's wife sits on every couch and makes the same look, as if she's offended or as if the couch has lied to her. "Well, it sort of has," she says. "You have to imagine you're not pregnant," Abbott keeps telling her. "I wish you knew what a ridiculous thing that is to say," she says. Abbott and his wife bicker all day and are constantly reminded of each other's most regrettable qualities. There are no good couches, but they pretend the real issue is their spouse's poor taste or unreasonable requirements. "Comfort is not an unreasonable requirement," Abbott's wife says, causing Abbott to wonder aloud whether they are wealthy enough for comfort. Abbott's daughter behaves like a two-year-old in a furniture store. She spills apple juice in a deluxe modern showroom, narrowly missing a divan. The child's stuffed pony is lost, discovered by a virtuous sales associate, then lost again. Abbott's wife's ankles hurt. She sits on couches and does not want to stand back up. The utopian community disintegrates, almost upon sunrise. All told, it lasted roughly thirteen hours, six of which Abbott spent sleeping. Like all other utopian settlements, including Robert Owen's New Harmony Community on the banks of the Wabash River in 1825, this La Quinta venture dissolves into chaos and fails. Still, Abbott considers while hiding from his family amidst the leather sectionals, all the *non*utopian communities have dissolved into chaos and failed, too. So big deal. So try again.

21 In Which Abbott Drives through the Center of a Diamond

Driving home, Abbott notices the sudden quiet in the backseat. The noticing perhaps more sudden than the quiet. By adjusting the rearview mirror he is able to see his two-year-old daughter and his substantially pregnant wife, both asleep, mouths parted, heads inclined toward each other. They are both a little sweaty and beautiful. By tilting the rearview even farther down—and by dropping his right shoulder nearly to discomfort—he is able to see his wife's breasts, enlarged by pregnancy and bisected intriguingly by her seatbelt. If seatbelts became standard in American cars in 1964, why, Abbott wonders—later, not now—is our contemporary national art not filled with breasts bisected by nylon straps? Where are the songs and poems, the sculpture, the oils on canvas? For a stretch of fifty or so highway miles, Abbott periodically readjusts his rearview mirror to look first at his sweet, sleeping family, then at his wife's splendid breasts. There is something here, inaccessible by blade, no matter how sharp. Although he is not generally a happy man—or perhaps *because* he is not generally a happy man—Abbott recognizes happiness when he feels it.

22 Abbott's Cave

Having not checked the Internet in nearly thirty hours, Abbott dials up with a premonition, though he also had a premonition the sun would rise this morning. Another full rotation of the planet—the odds of mayhem are pretty good. And sure enough: the steamboat has exploded; the gunman has walked in and opened fire; the gorillas in the zoo have stopped eating; and now these missing girls. Here's what we know: drunk babysitter, open screen door, tiny footprints in the mud. Authorities are amassing, combing, projecting. They are not answering that question at this time. They are utilizing all available resources. The parents are bargaining with God. "You shouldn't read that stuff," Abbott's wife has said, more or less concurring with Henry David Thoreau, who believed that anyone who cares to know that a man had his eyes gouged out this morning on the Wachito River is living in a cave, and not just any cave but a *dark unfathomed mammoth* one. Right now she's calling for Abbott from a remote region of the house. He understands her tone, if not her explicit message. When Abbott attempts to conclude his dial-up Internet session, he has, as always, a choice: STAY CONNECTED or DISCONNECT NOW.

23 Abbott's Folk Remedy

Abbott just stumbled accidentally upon this treatment, but now he swears by it. It's a little of the hair of the dog that bit you. The first thing you'll need to do is have a child. The best kind for this remedy is a child who has some manual dexterity, who can safely and neatly chew solid foods, and who can ride placidly in a car seat. A two-year-old child usually works well. Next you'll want to buckle the child into its car seat with some soothing words or perhaps a folk song about the sinking of a great ship. You don't want a fussy child. Start the car and begin driving around. It does not matter where you drive, but Abbott recommends, for safety's sake, that you avoid heavy traffic and/or winding roads. Also: a clear, dry day is best. Now, once you have helped create this child and buckled it happily into a moving car, you'll need to open a plastic bag full of snack items. Dry cereal is fine, as are raisins, pieces of dried fruit, or small nuts. Use something that the child likes. While steering with your left hand, use your right to offer a small snack item back to the child in the car seat. Show appropriate caution, obviously. Hold the snack item securely but gingerly. Do not turn around, and do not use the rearview mirror to look at the child. Looking back is not only dangerous, it also ruins the treatment. Keep your right hand extended backwards, despite the growing discomfort. If it helps, talk to the child about what is happening. ("Here's a pretzel for you.") *Now wait.* Keep your eyes on the road, your left hand on the wheel. Keep your snack arm extended toward the backseat. You may feel a burning sensation in your shoulder, and that's fine. Wait. Stop talking. The waiting is crucial. Your sense that the child does not want the snack item or can't reach it or in fact is not a real and separate person—crucial. Do not turn around. Do not talk. Just pose a question with your right arm, extend it into the mystery of the backseat. Now: Feel the child's tiny warm hand graze your scarred and callused fingers. This is important. Feel the child achieve a grip on the snack. Don't look! If you see it, you won't feel it. Feel the tug as the child, of its own startling volition, takes the food from your light grasp and, one presumes, eats it. Your snack hand should be and feel empty. The emptiness is crucial. Repeat as desired.

24 On Turbulence

It's nearly midnight when Abbott's wife walks into the basement to find Abbott with his head against a heating duct. She's holding a magazine, wearing underwear and a tank top that doesn't quite cover her stomach. Abbott can see a crescent of taut white skin beneath the hem. "What are you doing?" he says. "I've been looking all over for you," she says. "We should probably whisper," Abbott says, pointing upward. They are standing directly below their daughter's bedroom, and sound does carry in the house. Still, Abbott's wife rolls her eyes at him. "What are you doing?" she says. "Sorry you're still up," he says, putting his head against another section of duct. "This floor is gross," she says, and they both look down at her bare feet, one on top of the other, toes curled. Abbott's wife has to lean forward to see them. "I'm looking for a noise," he says. "What kind of noise?" "I don't know," he says. "Kind of a rustle. Tell me if you hear it." His wife switches feet. "I brought you something," she says. She opens the magazine and begins reading an article on airplane safety. She knows he is scared to fly, and she knows, further, that he reaches irritably after fact and reason. The chance of a plane crashing is one in 11 million.

The wings on a jet are built to flap up and down. It's called flexing. "I knew that one," Abbott says, tapping the edge of square silver duct with his fingernail. "And if the wings didn't flex, the ride would be terrible," his wife says. "I know," he says. His wife keeps reading. Only one plane has ever crashed because of turbulence. "*Ever?*" asks Abbott. "Ever," she says. "And probably only because it was flying too close to a mountain." Abbott's wife reads a passage about how people who are afraid of flying are advised to think about the plane being suspended in a big bubble of gelatin. Abbott has no idea what that means or how it might help. "And listen, turbulence," she says. "Turbulence, because of the speed of the air-craft, turbulence feels much worse than it actually is." Abbott stands up straight. The only light is from an exposed sixty-watt bulb on the ceiling. The basement darkens at the corners. His wife looks like some kind of ghost or dream, talking about aircraft. Abbott has cobwebs in his hair and on the back of his neck. "That doesn't make any sense," he says. "How can turbulence be not as bad as it feels? Turbulence *is* what turbulence feels like. That's exactly what it is. You can't distinguish turbulence from its effects." "No," his wife says. "There's the air currents or whatever outside the plane. Think of the gelatin. Then there's the bumping and falling sen-sation that the passengers experience." "We should whisper," Abbott says. "I might have just heard the rustle," she says. "That wasn't it," he says. "If you hit a tiny rock in a car going thirty miles per hour, it doesn't feel that bad, but if you hit the same kind of bump in a jet going"—she checks the magazine—"eight hundred feet per second, then it feels more severe." Ab-bott is almost entirely certain that an airplane would not hit a tiny rock in the air, though he wishes his wife had clarified that point. She says, "Not that planes hit rocks. They hit air currents." "Of course," Abbott says. He had never considered that turbulence exists independently of our percep-tion of it, though the point is suddenly evident. "The main thing is if you can picture the aircraft in a big pocket of gelatin," she says. "I still don't get that," Abbott says. He would like to get it. "A jet is only moving about one inch up or down," she says. She has closed the magazine, and she is palpating herself below the ribs. "Are you OK?" Abbott says. His wife says, "The baby keeps jabbing me up here." He says, "Are you worried about it?" She says, "No. The main point with the turbulence is that things aren't really as bad as they seem. Or feel." Neither Abbott nor his wife says anything for a minute or so. There is no need for Abbott's wife to say that turbulence is in this respect just like so many things in life, and there's no need for Abbott to say that turbulence is in this respect quite exceptional. At some point you do not need to talk to have a conversation. The conversation exists whether you have it or not. It continues silently in a parallel dimension of the marriage. They both pause to let it run its course toward another stalemate. When it's over, Abbott whispers, "Eight hundred feet per second?"

25 The Obstetrician's Tale

"It's a true story. During my first pregnancy, I really did stay up late at night reading my old embryology textbook—those million tiny things that all have to happen perfectly. And I really did come in to work early every day to give myself an ultrasound. I'm only trying to commiserate, but I should know by now that there are some people—and it's usually the men—who I just shouldn't say those things to." "But still . . ." "Still what? It's nice that they come?" "Well, it *is* nice." "You know, I used to think that too. But now I'm sick of all these heroes."

26 Abbott and the Oversized Load

Abbott empties the dirty water from his daughter's inflatable pool by stepping on the edge. When all the water has drained into the yard, he uses his hose and hose attachment to spray out the dead bugs and blades of grass from the bottom and sides. Today it is above ninety degrees. He drags the pool ten feet away so he won't kill the grass beneath it. It might be too late for that, he speculates. After he locates the two valves and blows in more air, he removes the hose attachment and places the running hose in the pool. The water from the hose is too cold for his daughter, though, so Abbott boils water in a teakettle on the stove, then takes the kettle outside with an oven mitt and pours it into the pool. He pours in four kettles of boiling water. Abbott's daughter will be excited. Abbott moves a deck chair to the edge of the pool, where he might sit this afternoon with his feet in the water. When the girl awakes from her nap, she does not want to play in the pool. She wants to walk. She and Abbott walk through the neighborhood to a busy street called Pleasant. Abbott picks her up, and they watch the traffic pass. The girl is quiet, lethargic. Abbott puts his palm on her forehead—of course she feels hot. He puts his palm on his own hot forehead and determines nothing. They see delivery trucks, a motorcycle, a town bus. Then Abbott points and says, "Look at that. Right there, coming this way." The girl turns her head toward the flatbed tractor-trailer carrying a small white house. In front of the truck there's an escort car with a yellow flashing light on its roof. The house on the truck passes slowly by. "Pretty amazing," Abbott says to her, before noticing that she's crying. She's not making a sound. Tears are filling her eyes and running down her cheeks and neck. "It's OK," Abbott tells her. "Let's go get a snack." He carries her back down the street toward their house. She smells like sunblock. "Listen," he says, "it's just fine." Tonight he'll tell his wife about it. One of them will say it's troubling. The other will say it's nothing to worry about. Abbott doesn't know yet which one he'll be.

27 In Which Abbott Sits in a Parked Car for Quite a While

Were he to marry, twenty-eight-year-old Charles Darwin scribbled in pencil on the backs of envelopes, he would never see America; he would never learn French; he would never go up in a hot air balloon; he would never take a *solitary trip in Wales;* he would be obliged to go walking every day with his wife; he would be forced to visit and receive relatives; he would be forced to *bend in every trifle;* he could not read in the evenings; he would be fat and idle, anxious and responsible; he would never have enough money for books; he would be banished from London; he would be trapped in London; he would have the expense and worry of children; he would feel a duty to work for money, especially if he had many children; he would be forced to host visitors and be a part of Society; he would listen to *female chit-chat;* he would have no time in the country, no tours; he would have no large zoological collection; he would not have enough books; he would have no freedom to go where he liked; he would not have the *conversation of clever men at clubs;* he would suffer, above all else, a *terrible loss of time.* Darwin was married within the year. He and his wife, Emma Wedgwood Darwin, produced ten children, three of whom died young. Late in life, he wrote of Emma: "She has been my greatest blessing, and I can declare that in my whole life I have never heard her utter one word which I had rather have been unsaid. . . . I marvel at my good fortune that she, so infinitely my superior in every single moral quality, consented to be my wife. She has been my wise adviser and cheerful comforter throughout life." And to his children Darwin wrote: "I have indeed been most happy in my family, and I must say to you children that not one of you has ever given me one minute's anxiety, except on the score of health. . . . When you were very young it was my delight to play with you all, and I think with a sigh that such days can never return."

28 Abbott and the Vexing Claims of Purity

Furthermore, Abbott's daughter will not drink her organic cow's milk.
Just will *not*, no matter how many times her father takes a sip of it and
then licks his lips and rubs his belly. Then this morning Abbott's wife
has what she considers a breakthrough when she adds maple syrup to the
milk and the child drinks it eagerly. "Maple milk!" his wife says, making
lip-smacking noises at the child. Abbott is not impressed. He feels his
belly-rubbing program has not been given enough time to succeed. "And
all those additives and chemicals," he says to his wife. "No," she says, "it's
pure maple syrup." "Right, *pure*," Abbott says, troubled by the stupidity of
his sarcasm. He gets up from his chair and walks to the kitchen to scruti-
nize the syrup bottle, which does indeed disingenuously announce its 100
percent purity. What he will do, he decides, is read the ingredients out
loud like the Declaration of Independence, but he finds upon inspection
that the ingredients are not listed on the bottle, so his scheme collapses.
"I thought they were required to put the ingredients on here," he says.
"What?" his wife says. "It's pure maple syrup. *Sap*, that's the ingredient.
Look at her go." There's no denying it, the child is crazy about maple

milk. Abbott is still perplexed by the absent list of ingredients. "Syrup is not sap," he says with a derisiveness born of uncertainty. "It can't just be sap." His voice nearly cracks, and his wife turns in her chair to face him. "Well, what do you think it is?" she says, laughing now. "Processed sugar," he says. "And aspartame. Lead paint. Fluorocarbons. Agent Orange. Parablendeum. How does it get so delicious?" "More?" Abbott's daughter says, holding up her empty cup. "They do something to it," his wife says, "but they don't add anything. I'm not saying it's health food, but I know it's natural. Pure Vermont maple syrup—what did you think that meant?" Abbott disappears into his office, where, after establishing a particularly strong dial-up Internet connection, he learns, at age thirty-seven, that real maple syrup is, after all, just maple sap—from a tree—boiled down. (Native Americans taught the early settlers how to make it. For a sugar maple tree, you'll need about thirty-two gallons of sap to make a gallon of syrup. It's a good idea to strain the finished syrup through cheesecloth to remove any debris or crystallized minerals.) Here he is, suspicious of trees. He hunches over the laptop in his darkened office, chastened and contrite. Outside, someone is mowing in the rain. Abbott knows you can't just believe. He knows you can't just not believe.

29 Abbott and the Infestation

Every Sunday morning Abbott retrieves from the end of the driveway a newspaper in a blue plastic bag. Every Sunday morning he pulls the plastic bag off the newspaper and drops it into a low kitchen drawer containing nothing but blue plastic bags. This morning he opens the drawer with his foot and tosses the balled-up bag into the drawer, which is, Abbott now sees, filled completely with blue plastic bags. This morning's blue bag falls slowly onto the pile, then slides and tumbles out of the drawer and onto the kitchen floor. It stretches out nearly to full length. A draft of air nudges it across the tile. Abbott's dog jumps back and yelps, in all likelihood waking the child. Abbott looks down into the heaping drawer of weeks. This is how you know that you have Time in your house; you discover its shed skins. He places the thick newspaper on the counter, where it will remain until it is recycled. He gets down on his knees by the drawer. Who else is going to do it? He opens a blue plastic bag and begins to shove the other blue bags into it. The opening is small, so the work is painstaking. When he's finished, he ties the top of the bulging bag in a knot and tosses the whole year into the garage. Today he'll deal with shit, snot, piss, blood, vomit, rust, and rot, but they won't be bad in quite the same way that this is bad.

30 On Conservation

All day long Abbott and his wife have been arguing. By evening there is a fragile truce. The daughter has been put to bed, though her singing and babbling are audible on the staticky monitor. "I forgot to even ask you about the butterflies," Abbott's wife says, conciliatory in word if not tone. They are together in the family room, a designation they actually use. They are sitting as far apart as possible on the devastated couch, purchased at a furniture warehouse years ago, when Abbott was in graduate school, and now draped like a corpse by a mail-order cover. Besides Abbott's cocktail, the couch is the only adult item in the family room, which this and every evening looks as though robbers have ransacked it in an urgent search for a small and valuable item. Books, toys, coins, buttons, beads, and costume jewelry lie strewn across the stained carpeting. It's almost impossible not to fight with your life partner in this room. Abbott's wife has asked, sort of, about Abbott's trip to the butterfly conservatory, an outing he took this morning with their daughter but did not discuss afterward with his wife because she was too busy reminding him of things about which he did not need to be reminded. Today was Abbott's first trip to the butterfly conservatory. His wife has been twice before with their daughter, and she has reported that the conservatory is "neat" and "kind of peaceful," that it's "an interesting place in the middle of nowhere." One response to his wife's inquiry is that the butterfly conservatory is a hideous travesty, a transparent example of everything that is wrong with everything. The twelve-dollar admission, accepted joylessly by a woman talking on the telephone to someone she clearly does not want in her life anymore; the cruel trap of the overstocked gift shop, selling stuffed butterflies, real butterflies, butterfly magnets and puzzles, butterfly nightlights and kites, along with entire aisles of bright toys thematically irrelevant but wildly attractive to children; the children; the lucrative imprisonment of thousands of butterflies, not to mention finches, turtles, lizards, fish, and a parrot, ostensibly in the name of appreciation and education; the *heat,* as one might find in a small bathroom after a long hot shower; the horrific music—hyperactive, flute-driven renditions of "Edelweiss" and "On Broadway," engineered to overpower visitors and create in them a stupor that might be mistaken for relaxation; the weird smell; the cafeteria with its dumb food names; the fellow adult patrons, all behaving as though they have never before encountered a flying insect; the pervasive sense of animal dirtiness; the chipper, ecologically ignorant staff members, who are in all seriousness referred to as *flight attendants,* and who spend their days trying to get children to pet a sleepy lizard—Abbott ponders this truce-obliterating response. It would no doubt feel good to take a big swing. But the truth is, he had a pretty good time at the conservatory. There were so many butterflies. Some landed on people's hands or shoulders. The large proboscises were easy to see. Butterflies are astonishing when you look at them, and when else would you ever look at them? The flight attendants had helpfully led Abbott and his daughter to a mounted board of cocoons, where they saw butterflies emerging, drying their wings, then flying off into the world, or at least into the hot dome. Abbott had never seen his daughter so engaged, so stimulated. He knows that the conservatory is, in addition to a hideous travesty, something like a spiritual center, operated by a dedicated team of citizen-workers. Who else cares about butterflies? Who else would attempt to mend their broken wings with a special wing glue? The pop of the ice in Abbott's glass reminds him—and probably his wife—that he has not, as a courtesy, desisted or at least curtailed his drinking during her pregnancy. This is a courtesy extended by quite a few Pioneer Valley men to their pregnant soul mates. Abbott has still not said a word in response to his wife's question, which, come to think of it, was not so much a question as a statement about forgetting to ask a question. His eyes are on a section of subtoy carpet in the shape of a rhombus. Either a rhombus or a parallelogram. He knows that any criticism of the butterfly conservatory would be a deliberate attempt to rankle his wife and renew the fight. This is what a married person can do, slander a sanctuary to provoke his beloved. But Abbott does not disparage the conservatory or its workers. His decision not to strikes him as exceedingly mature, though he knows that congratulating oneself on one's maturity is probably immature. Also, it comes as a tremendous disappointment to Abbott that his wife cannot know his restraint. If she could know, she would be touched. But he can't very well tell her how mature and restrained he's acting, for the maturity and restraint would evaporate upon utterance. Abbott and his wife can hear their daughter, through the monitor, singing an Australian folk song about a swagman who drowns himself in the billabong. She's waiting for an answer, his wife is. She's been waiting this whole time. Abbott clenches his jaw, stares at the dirty rhombus. When it comes down to it, he cannot bring himself to say that the butterfly conservatory was amazing, or even that it was neat, even though it would be at least partially true and would help salvage the evening. This is another small failure of spirit, and he knows it. The knowing of it might make things better, but probably makes things much, much worse. "It was fine," he says of his outing with their daughter. And then he repeats it: "It was fine." This is either an act of aggression or diplomacy, he's not sure which at this point. His wife is a separate person, large on the inside, capable of a very broad range of responses. She folds her thin fingers across her belly and gets ready to say something.

31 The Brave Simplicity of Truth

Death is the muse of Stupid Thoughts. Here's one: "Maybe we'll see some good names for the baby," Abbott had told his wife as they parked the car by the old New England cemetery. Here's another: Perhaps the high infant mortality rate in early America made parents more temperate in their love of children. The grass is already beginning to fade and wilt. Grasshoppers shoot from the lawn like fireworks. There, at the end of the row, is the infant son of Cotton and Euphrenia—*8d* must mean eight days. Out on the street, the cars move swiftly past. Meanwhile, Abbott's daughter has found a heart-shaped headstone, and she's racing back and forth from it to Abbott's wife. The headstone is chipped and mossy, like a heart should be. "Touch the heart!" she yells. "Touch the heart!" Her hair is wet and curly in the heat. She has two Band-Aids on her knee. Abbott's wife bends to read stones. She's pregnant in a graveyard, for God's sake. Abbott considers a satirical remark, but he keeps his mouth shut for reasons unknown to him but not unknown to James Russell Lowell, also dead. "Truth is quite beyond the reach of satire," wrote Lowell, while alive. "There is so brave a simplicity in her, that she can no more be made ridiculous than oak or pine." The graves stretch for acres beneath the sun. Somewhere nearby, someone must be burning brush. Abbott bounces on the balls of his feet, twists his trunk until his vertebrae crack. He regards the narrow stretch of freshly mown grass before him. Stupidity, morbidity, irony . . . that leaves only gymnastics. "Honey!" he shouts at his daughter. "Honey, check out Dad."

August

1 Abbott and the Clogged Main

This morning there is quite a bit of water on the basement floor, so Abbott checks the Internet. He flushes the toilet and then scrambles downstairs to see more water spilling from what he thinks are called pipe joints. What he has, according to the Internet, is a clog. He consults the Yellow Pages, trying to determine, based exclusively on fonts, graphics, and slogans, which plumbing companies provide prompt service and excellent work at a reasonable price. They all do, apparently, though most of them use strange quotation marks. One advertisement for a local, family-operated business features a smiling, large-headed cartoon plumber clutching an enormous wrench and sprinting clogward, trailed by the lines that universally denote alacrity. This looks good to Abbott, and so he calls. He is handling this problem. He is taking care of his house and family. His wife and daughter went to Story Time at the public library, and they are due to return in forty-five minutes. Abbott's wife's dismay about the clog and its consequences in a one-toilet home will be attenuated, Abbott suspects, by her discovery of his swift and frugal decision making. The nice woman who answers the family-operated plumbing business's phone asks if it's the main line that's clogged. Abbott breathes into the receiver. For an instant he considers terminating the call. The woman says, "Is it the big pipe, do you think? The four-inch one?" Abbott walks downstairs with the phone and a tape measure. The woman waits patiently. He surveys the plumbing, the impressive copper network. He has not been adequately respectful of and grateful for this system, he knows. He traces the route of the water, considers the location of the leaky joints. Yes, he tells the nice woman, he thinks it's the main pipe. "Well," she says, "we don't have that big a snake." Abbott does not understand what she's talking about. "I see," he says. "We can only clean out a two-inch pipe," she says, "but I can give you the name of a pipe rooter who can take care of you. He's the best there is." Abbott is impressed by her generosity and her loyalty, and he is proud to have located, through his own initiative, the best pipe rooter out there. He takes down the name and number. "Thank you so much," he says. "Have a nice day," she says. Under normal circumstances, Abbott would take a short break between phone calls, but currently he is feeling hale and capable, and so he immediately calls the vaunted Pipe Rooter. After four rings, he reaches an automated system and he is asked to leave a voice message. He ends the call, paces the wet basement floor, and constructs in his mind a succinct, forceful, and informative message about the pipe and the clog. Then he takes a deep breath, and he calls the Pipe Rooter again. This time the Pipe Rooter answers after one ring, flustering Abbott beyond hope of recovery. "Yeah," the Pipe Rooter says, by way of salutation. "Hello?" Abbott says, considering whether to hang up. "Yeah?" says the Pipe Rooter. "I was going to leave a message about my clog," Abbott says. "Clogged main?" the Pipe Rooter says. "My main line is clogged," Abbott says, "and the plumber I talked to isn't able to handle the width of the pipe." Abbott does not want to mention the snake if he can help it, because it's lewd and because he is not sure he heard the woman correctly. "Yeah, you'll need a big snake for that," the Pipe Rooter says. "That's what I understand," Abbott says. The Pipe Rooter asks Abbott for his address, and Abbott supplies the proper answer. The Pipe Rooter says, "I actually have a little time right now if that works." Abbott is thrilled by the promptness, but the thrill soon fades to distress. If he arranges and then supervises the repair before his wife is even aware of the problem, then she will never understand and appreciate his role in the crisis. She'll return to the house to learn that the main line was clogged and then fixed. It will be like it all never happened. The toilet worked when she left, and it will work when she returns, a scenario that dismays Abbott. He might as well tell her the roof blew off and he put on a new one. She'll be left with a bill but with no real sense of the privation or exigency, or of his competent response. "Take your time," Abbott says. "I'm on my way," the Pipe Rooter says. "You come highly recommended," Abbott says. "Just open the bulkhead, if you don't mind, and I can get started right away," the Pipe Rooter says. Ten minutes later, the Pipe Rooter's van is in Abbott's driveway, and the Pipe Rooter is dragging his equipment around to the back. He is probably sixty years old, gray-haired and ruddy. Through the kitchen window Abbott watches him descend into the bulkhead. Then Abbott walks downstairs to the basement. The Pipe Rooter is crouched behind the washing machine, and Abbott lingers silently across the room. The Pipe Rooter stands and puts a large red hand on top of the washer. "My kids never liked those things," the Pipe Rooter says, pointing to a dismantled swing chair against the wall. "When I swung them myself, they loved it, but then as soon as I put them in the chair, they'd wail." Abbott nods. "But my grandkids love that stuff," the Pipe Rooter says. Abbott asks how many grandchildren the Pipe Rooter has. "Four," he says. "And two are living with us now because their mom just got a divorce and she's trying to get back on her feet. She got married young. So now she's got to find herself. I told her, 'Shit, you think your parents' house is the place to look?'" "Right," Abbott says. "The little ones are fun to have around, but they're wild. It's been a long time since we've had kids in the house. I'd forgotten what it's like. It's terrible. My wife remembered, but I didn't." The Pipe Rooter laughs. "It's pretty bad," Abbott says. "It's a blessing, though," the Pipe Rooter says. He crouches again behind the washer. If his daughter misbehaves at Story Time, Abbott thinks, perhaps his wife will return early. "I remember this house," the Pipe Rooter says. "I've been out here a couple times over the years. The snake goes out about ninety feet and there's a place where the big blade won't go through. I think the pipes out there under the road aren't quite matching up." He stands up and makes his hands into mismatched pipes for Abbott. "Maybe a busted coupling, maybe some roots coming through. So I'll bring the snake out that far and use the smaller blade. Should take about twenty minutes is all." Abbott says, "It just goes in there like that?" "Just like that," the Pipe Rooter says. The sun shines through the bulkhead and makes a golden rectangle on the cement. "Let me know when you're done, and I'll write you a check," Abbott says. "I was here in this house maybe ten or twelve years ago," the Pipe Rooter says. He breathes heavily as he turns his wrench. "I'll never forget it. See how you've got this open drain in the floor here?" Abbott walks across the basement and peers behind the washing machine. "I was down here working just like I am now. I kept hearing this little chirping noise, and I couldn't figure out where it was coming from. Then when I was packing up my tools, this little bird flew out of the drain. Right there." The Pipe Rooter points with his wrench. "Flew right past me, out the bulkhead, into the sky. Scared me to death. Just a little brown bird, like a swallow. I told the guy who lived here, and I could tell he didn't believe me. Hell, if I were you I wouldn't believe me either, but I saw it and it's true."

2 In Which There Are No Hard Feelings

Just this morning Abbott came up behind his wife while she was at the electric range, and he put his arms around the hard lower slope of her belly. She did not lean back into him, and she did not make that small, wonderful sound from the back of her throat. She did not stop tending her omelet. And now, hours later, she leans over the wobbly arm of the couch, trying to kiss him while he reads, but Abbott closes neither his eyes nor his big book.

3 Abbott and the Good News First

At the end of the day, after helping his wife get their daughter to bed, Abbott lies facedown on the carpet of the family room. He is unclean and unshaven. He knows not the date. His joints ache from what the Internet has diagnosed as either hepatitis or Lyme Disease. There is something (is it Yellow Turtle?) jutting into his ribs. Still, that old-time languor does not descend. He rolls over onto his back, regards the pattern of paint and texture on the ceiling. The pattern of paint and texture he finds uninteresting. Abbott recalls the hours spent lying on floors, staring at ceilings, awaiting a *feeling*, any feeling at all. (The music from a band that tuned its guitars irregularly.) He remembers the moves—high chin, slow blink, heavy arms out in Savior or up in Surrender—but the moves don't feel natural. Abbott is—tonight it's evident—no longer listless. He's bored, angry, exasperated, worried, gloomy, tired, sad, hot, afraid, and content, but not listless. Moreover, he's hungry. He gets off the floor, puts a doll where she goes, and walks to the kitchen.

4 Abbott at the Edge of His Seat

"I just pray this one is a good sleeper," Abbott's wife says, pointing to her abdomen. "Well," Abbott says, "the big sister was not too bad." This morning they are up before their daughter, and it is amazing. Abbott is happy and optimistic, though lurking at the far edge of his contentment is the knowledge that the coffeepot is almost empty. There might be enough for another half cup. "Are you kidding?" his wife says. "She was terrible. Completely terrible." "I mean, she wasn't great," Abbott says. "You don't remember?" his wife says. Abbott smiles in the manner of someone whose personality has been drastically altered by head injury. Abbott's wife always wants to know why there are long drips of coffee on the outside of Abbott's mug. He says the mug rims are too thick, but the real answer, he suspects, is that he is gulping the coffee. "She was a monster," Abbott's wife says. "There was that stretch where you had to take her out in the car to get her to sleep." Abbott's memory is stirred very lightly. "Oh, yeah," he says, "I remember doing that a few times." Abbott's wife says, "A few times? You did it every night for five weeks." Abbott envisions himself driving through the foothills of the Rockies with a sleeping infant in the backseat. It's not quite a memory, but it's a nice image. Still, he understands that you couldn't see Pikes Peak or Mt. Cheyenne because it would be dark outside. And also, there's NORAD. "Did I like doing that?" Abbott asks. "You mean driving around with her?" "Yeah." "I don't think so," she says. "And that one time you were gone for nearly an hour, and I was almost puking I was so worried. My breasts hurt, and my incision still hurt. Remember that? I was still having that feeling like my guts were shifting around. I was supposed to be getting some sleep while you were out, but I was pacing around the house, wondering what I would do if both of you were dead." Abbott pauses at this fork in the story. He can choose. He says, "What happened to us?" His wife laughs. Abbott says, "No, I mean where were we that night? Why were we so late?" "You honestly don't remember?" his wife says. Abbott shakes his head. He remembers now, but he wants to hear it from her. "First you got stuck at a train crossing. It was a long train, and then something happened to it." "Oh, yeah," Abbott says. "It just stopped." "And of course when the car stopped moving she woke up and started screaming." Abbott says, "Oh, man." "It was a long time," Abbott's wife says, "and when it finally moved, you were trying to rush home and you got pulled over by that cop." "You've got to be kidding," Abbott says. "He pulled you over because our front headlight was out." "I do remember that headlight," Abbott says. "And remember, you bought a headlight, and you kept saying you were going to put it in yourself because you weren't going to pay someone else to replace a stupid headlight, which is what we ended up doing." "But I don't think I got a ticket," Abbott says. "No, because the officer said he had a little one at home about the same age. You two had a little moment. You shook hands and agreed that there wasn't any sound worse than that." "And then what happened?" Abbott says. "And then you finally came home," his wife says. "When I heard the car pull up outside—I had actually been praying. Like actually saying a prayer." Abbott says, "Was she asleep?" His wife says, "She was going insane. And she was hoarse by then. And you—I've never seen you look like that. You were like some kind of POW." Abbott drops his head, rubs his palms on his knees. "I can only imagine," he says.

5 Abbott's Set Point

Right there on the brick wall of a Pioneer Valley bakery: HERE. WE.
COME. DEVILS. The spray-painted letters are eerily neat and uniform,
and the punctuation is terrifying. Had the vandal chosen a comma for
direct address, the effect would have been lost. And then that ominous
first-person plural . . . Everything about these words is calculated to
inspire dread. All day long Abbott has been rattled by the bakery graffiti.
This is no time for procreation, no time to make something that can get
hurt. Late tonight, on a whim, Abbott types "here we come devils" into
a dog-themed search engine and then clicks FETCH! The search turns
up twenty-three thousand hits. Abbott learns that the phrase is featured
loudly in a video game based on the career of General George Armstrong
Custer (1839–1876), infamous American cavalry commander and Indian
fighter who lost his life at Little Big Horn. Custer in Internet photographs
has the kind of droopy, creeping mustache that obscures the mouth.
Abbott is nearly giddy with the information. He feels emancipated. He
wants to go look at his sleeping daughter and put his hand on her head
again, but his wife has asked him to stop doing that because it disrupts

the child's sleep. He stays in his chair for quite some time, considering whether to assemble the crib, the pieces of which are stacked against the bookcase. A scrap of paper on the desk by the laptop is blank except for the word *rash*. Gradually, Abbott becomes less sanguine. Gradually, he returns to his prior state of agitation, what researchers might call his *set point*. The problem, Abbott realizes, is that the bakery graffiti signifies exactly what he thought it signifies.

6 Abbott near the Doorway

Abbott's unborn child's head is still facing the wrong direction, and his wife is quiet the entire ride home from the obstetrician's office. "Maybe it will still flip," Abbott says as his family lingers in the car in the driveway. "Or it won't," she says. Later, he finds her sitting in a chair she never sits in, her hair over her eyes. Nobody ever sits in this chair. "I'm sorry," he says. He offers to turn on a light, not because it is dark in the room but because it would give him something to do. "Are you crying?" Abbott says. He stands near the doorway, ten feet from his wife. His impulse to leave the room prevents him from approaching his wife's chair. His impulse to approach his wife's chair prevents him from leaving the room. The countervailing desires create in him a radical stillness. He is near the doorway but not in it. Both his feet are on the rug. His arms hang loose at his sides. "I'm sorry," he says again. Abbott's wife says, "I was just thinking of a story about this guy I once knew. He told me that one time when he was eight or nine he had a horrible earache during a sleepover at a friend's house, and he didn't want to wake anyone up, so he just lay there and suffered all night. He said it was excruciating. He said he just gripped the side of his head and rolled around in bed, whispering for help, hoping his friend would wake up, but he didn't. It turned out to be a bad infection." The phone rings once and then stops. Abbott looks down at his wife, who is looking through the window at whatever can be seen from the chair. The wind has picked up. "Who knows what made me think of that," she says. "Isn't it awful, though?"

7 Abbott and the Visiting Nurse

The change to Abbott's life-insurance policy requires that a nurse visit his home to make sure he is not about to perish. She arrives this morning, right on time, carrying a large black bag. She moves up the driveway like a blade. What Abbott knows about nurses is that they are honed to a sharp edge. They don't get paid enough, they work weird hours, they lift heavy things, they get dirty. They deal with ridiculous doctors and ridiculous patients within a ridiculous health care system. They've seen it all. Nobody appreciates them. They are righteously aggrieved. They have strong opinions, which they voice as facts. They develop their own strange, contradictory, and wildly divergent theories of well-being, illness, and recovery. They smoke. They are disgruntled, and their disgruntlement gives them purpose, energy, a quick step. They are not hopeful or cheerful or optimistic—just competent. Abbott admires them quite a bit, though naturally he is scared of them. First, Abbott and the nurse fill out paperwork at the dining-room table. Abbott reviews the policy. He understands that he can't commit suicide for two years, and he initials. He understands, at least vaguely, what "the death of the policyholder" means. He understands they'll be checking his blood for the very worst diseases. The thought is so sad Abbott can barely remain seated. It's nearly impossible to imagine not being there to watch your children grow up. It seems easy to imagine, but when you imagine them without you, you imagine it as if you're still watching from behind a tree or within a closet with the door cracked. The nurse pulls a scale from her bag, and Abbott steps on it. She measures his waist size. "What do you teach?" she says, and Abbott tells her. "Oh, God," she says, laughing. Her hands are powerful. She smells like cigarettes. "Go pee," she says, "and just leave this cup in there." Abbott pees in the cup and leaves it in the bathroom. The nurse has been here less than ten minutes, and she has already made him feel like a visitor in his own house. When he comes back, she goes to the bathroom to handle his urine. Abbott hears the flush of the toilet. She returns to take his blood pressure and pulse. When she breaks the seal on a plastic bag and removes a needle, Abbott extends his arm across the table and turns away. "You're one of those?" the nurse says. Abbott says, "I'd just rather not look." The nurse begins a conversation to get him to relax. She talks about all these campus shootings. The guns, the mental illness. She asks if the university has been running any workshops or drills. She puts the needle in his arm. "I think so," Abbott says. He looks out at the street, where three neighbors are talking and pointing up at something on a house—a gutter or a chimney. Abbott can hear the shouts of children, the rhythmic creak of a metal swing set. "I worry about society," the nurse says, removing the needle from Abbott's arm. He turns and sees the dark vial. "You know?" she says. "Society is just getting worse and worse." This notion is central to Abbott's identity. He has held it for many years. For a long time it was a way to choose friends and television programs. It was something like an animating force. It wasn't necessarily that he wanted Society to be getting worse and worse, but the undeniable worsening of Society gave him a way to be in the world. "I think you're right," he tells the nurse. He still believes it. The difference now, though, is that he wishes he didn't.

8 Abbott Concedes

Unconsciousness, however, eradicates the possibility of surprise. A man who remains conscious may find himself living a day he never imagined, various elements of his life coalescing, like words in a sentence, to create something new and fantastical. For instance, tonight Abbott bathes his young daughter, puts her to bed, and then bathes his wife. (Her hair, enhanced by pregnancy, is a gleaming rope. The shampoo he rinses with an orange cup shaped like an elephant.)

9 Discretion Is the Better Part of Discreteness

It came as a revelation to Abbott when, several nights ago, he gleaned from an offhand remark of his wife's that the tomatoes the family has been enjoying this summer are not from the grocery store but from some private residence on Rolling Ridge Drive, about a mile away from Abbott's house. He found it simultaneously threatening and spiritually arousing that his pregnant wife could have been buying produce out of some vegetable gardener's driveway for weeks without his knowledge. It wasn't quite jealousy. It was the shocking autonomy of the loved one. "Is it like some kind of farmer's stand?" he asked, trying to comprehend. "Or produce stand?" "No," she said, with a nonchalance that may or may not have been feigned. "Just people. People with a card table." Abbott then requested, with the firmness of a demand, that he accompany his wife the next time she buys tomatoes "right off the street." "OK," she said. "Sure." So here we are, a sunny late morning in which Abbott drives his wife and daughter to Rolling Ridge Drive for tomatoes. On the way, Abbott learns that his wife has been making this trip on foot for most of the summer, but the heat and advanced pregnancy now make it difficult to walk. "So you drive?" Abbott asks. "Yes," she says. "How many times?" he says.

"What does it matter?" she asks. "A ballpark figure," he says. Abbott's wife says, "I don't know. Four? Five?" (What must be most disconcerting to a spouse about a private investigator's manila envelope of telephotographs, Abbott thinks—but certainly not right now—is not the demonstration of infidelity but the demonstration of separateness.) Abbott considers asking why she never told him about the tomatoes, but he does not. He wonders why he has not once seen his wife enter the house with a bag of tomatoes. Has he been that dazed and inattentive? Does he in a sense not *want* to see the bag of tomatoes? Or has she been sneaking the tomatoes into the house? These tomatoes—they are first-rate. Only a man desperate to believe they come from a grocery store could believe they come from a grocery store. "You might see a big black cat," Abbott's wife tells their daughter. "Sometimes there's a big cat." Abbott's wife's familiarity with the tomato vendor's pet does not sit well with Abbott. "Tractor," the girl says, transposing her adventures. And here they are in front of a split-level ranch on Rolling Ridge Drive. Abbott might have driven right past it had his wife not pointed it out. In the driveway there is indeed a card table, on top of which are small cartons of tomatoes and a sign too small to read from the road. Abbott takes his daughter out of her car seat. "Where is the proprietor?" asks Abbott. "They're usually not around," his wife says as she walks up the drive. All—or many—of Abbott's questions are answered when he approaches the card table, on which he sees not only the sign and the small cartons of tomatoes, but a stack of plastic bags pinned down by a rock and an old Folger's can with the lid on. The sign asks patrons please not to take the containers, but instead to put the tomatoes into one of the plastic bags beneath the rock. The sign also indicates that a carton costs two dollars, payable to the coffee can (in which a patron also might find ones to make change). Abbott's daughter is on the front porch of the ranch, squeezing the tail of an enormous black cat. Abbott's wife transfers two cartons of tomatoes to a bag, then returns the empty containers to the table. She takes the lid off the coffee can, puts in a five-dollar bill, and removes a dollar as change. She has obviously done this numerous times, perhaps nine or ten. Abbott can see quite a few bills at the bottom of the can. "So," Abbott's wife says, "this is it." Abbott collects his daughter and buckles her into her car seat. On the short ride home, all three members of the family are in high spirits. Abbott's wife loves these tomatoes. Abbott's daughter loves animals with furry tails. And Abbott loves the theory of human nature that the unattended coffee can allows him to cling to. If Abbott's wife has had occasion to speak to the elderly owners of the house and if she knows for a fact that thrice this summer some human has made off with the coffee can in broad daylight—the last of whom actually pelted the house with tomatoes before absconding—then that is something she keeps to herself.

10 Abbott's Reminder

Abbott occasionally forgets that pregnancy culminates in childbirth. More precisely, Abbott only occasionally remembers that pregnancy culminates in childbirth. Abbott's wife's gradual expansion, though, is indeed caused by a very small and helpless creature with no reasoning skills. As that creature grows, it will eat sand and develop ear infections. From time to time Abbott remembers, always with a sense of euphoric apprehension. This afternoon Abbott, his wife, and their daughter are visiting the hospital, or, in the idiom of third-trimester checklists, *touring the birthing facility*. Touring a birthing facility is, Abbott discovers, a powerful mnemonic. He can see the weary parents and grandparents walking the halls. The women, the new mothers, move slowly and clutch IV stands, medical carts, bassinets, or nurses. They don't clutch husbands. The husbands are useless. They are stranded in the old world, while the women clearly have visited a distant place on their own. And now they're back and their bodies are wrecked and their eyes have that unfocused look that seems to be less about fatigue than transcendence—as if conventional sense perception is no longer interesting or even necessary. The husbands are goofy and exalted, happy and proud. They are incapable of walking at the appropriate pace. They walk too far ahead of the women, and then they come back and walk too far behind them, and then they begin walking too far ahead again. In the nursery the swaddled newborns lie peacefully beneath heat lamps, giving the false impression that they are good. One opens its eyes slowly. "Baby," Abbott's daughter says as Abbott holds her up to the window. They tour the recovery room, the kitchen. Abbott is pleased to learn that the chair becomes a bed, that the refrigerator is open to fathers. "Same as the last time," Abbott's wife tells Abbott, and he nods as if he remembers. Every nurse talks to Abbott's daughter. "Look at you," they say. "Aren't you sweet." They give her stickers that say *I Was Brave* and *I'm a Big Sister*. Abbott's daughter peels the stickers and applies them to herself immediately. Roxanne, the nurse and tour guide, speaks only to Abbott's wife, as if Abbott does not understand the language. "You're cesarean, right?" Abbott's wife nods, and Abbott nods too. "OK," Roxanne says, "on the morning you come in, we'll set you up in a birthing room. We'll get you hooked to the monitor and get your vitals and prepare you for the section. We'll need to get a catheter in. You know about that, Mom. We'll put Dad in scrubs. Then we'll take you to the O.R. and start the anesthesia. You'll be awake the whole time, Mom. When that's ready, we'll come for Dad. After the delivery, we'll clean up the baby right there in the room. If everything is OK, we'll keep the little one in there with you. We don't split up mothers and babies if we don't have to. It's not like the old days. When they finish stitching you up, Mom, we'll take all of you to a different room for recovery. Do you have any questions?" Abbott's mind is a vast windy plain at dusk, swept clean of word and thought. "No," Abbott's wife says. "Great," says Roxanne. "We'll see you in a few weeks." Abbott tries to show his daughter the babies in the nursery once more, but this time the blinds are drawn. They leave the hospital then and go downtown for a large pizza.

11 Abbott's Inadvertent Research on Prepositions

Abbott mows the lawn, secretly enjoying himself. His wife and daughter play with sticks in the driveway. He cannot hear them over the sound of the mower, nor does he want to. The mown lines are green and fragrant; the robins drop into his wake for worms. The lawn is filled with weeds, but even weeds look good after mowing. This old mower just runs and runs. The blade is new and scrupulous. Abbott installed it an hour ago, lying beneath the propped mower, tightening the bolt with two hands, a grunt. At the end of a long row, he turns the mower back toward the house and sees that his wife and daughter are no longer in the driveway. They've probably gone back inside. Now the evening is still good, but not quite as good as it was.

12 In Which a Gorilla Appears

Actually, it appears to be a minimum-wage employee in a gorilla costume, but Abbott feels neither scorn nor pity nor melancholy. He's not speculating why it is that primates are comic, and he's not reflecting pensively about Dian Fossey or evolutionary branching. This is because he's with his daughter, and his daughter is, in the presence of the gorilla, enraptured. Just think about her afternoon. It begins with another rainy-day trip to the chain bookstore on Route 9, and suddenly it has a *gorilla* in it. And this gorilla appears to be improvising—it is bounding over children's tables, knocking down display books, and pounding its chest loudly, at least for a bookstore. Abbott's daughter stands with her fingers in her mouth, immobilized by ecstasy. She is a conductor. She conducts wonder. Wonder passes from the world to Abbott through his daughter. One could say that he is taking pleasure in the reckless bookstore gorilla, but he is not even looking at the reckless bookstore gorilla. He is looking at his daughter as she looks at the gorilla. Later—not now, thank goodness—Abbott will have to consider how it is possible that *watching* another person live so fully and directly can feel so powerfully like living fully and directly.

13 Abbott Makes a Move

Abbott and his wife walk toward each other in the cluttered family room, though they are not each other's destination. There is only one narrow path through the clutter. As they meet, Abbott turns sideways to the left to allow his wife to pass, and as she does, he grabs her right breast. In fairness, he means to caress her right breast, but it is difficult to caress a moving body part. If pressed, Abbott would be forced to admit that there is not one erotic aspect of this tableau. Not one. It's late morning, very hot. Abbott's wife is deep in the third trimester of a rough pregnancy. Their daughter is with them in the room, squeezing old bath water out of a lobster. Abbott is wearing what he wore yesterday, and perhaps the day before that. Abbott's wife laughs, but not in the right way. "What?" Abbott says, prepared to defend the indefensible. "I just don't know what you were hoping to accomplish," she says. Abbott does not know, either, so this conversation will have no brakes and no steering mechanism. "You just never know," he says, "when a little spark can start a fire." Despite the joke, he is not joking, which is to say his irony is ironic. "A fire?" she says. "Are you serious?" "Of course not," Abbott says. "Then what—" his wife begins, but she stops and begins again. "I think it's potentially sweet that you groped me," she says. "But I'm sorry, you are just not going to start a fire." She pulls her maternity blouse up over her stomach. There's a watermelon. It's her flesh, and it is exciting, but it is also looks at this point like a carnival exhibit. "This," she says, holding her belly like a big potted plant, "this is inflammable." "Right," Abbott says. He is not so dumb as to think now is a good time to bring up the quirky lexical item that *inflammable* is in fact a synonym, not an antonym, for *flammable*. You can look it up. And thus his wife has just unwittingly suggested her sexual readiness, her *combustibility*. Abbott's wife says, "She's not drinking from that lobster, is she?" Abbott, typically so heedful, is unconcerned. There is a quirky lexical item he is determined to share.

14 Abbott, Pierced by the Subjunctive

Not entirely sober, Abbott finds his wife standing at a living-room window that looks out upon what might initially appear to be a low bright moon, but which is in fact a yellow streetlight in a cloud of moths. Abbott is reminded, later, of something he once read: A human might mistake a rock for a bear, but never a bear for a rock. This is the type of window in front of which you might hold a crying infant. He puts his hands on his wife's shoulders, which neither relax nor tense. Indeed, it seems to Abbott that she has not noticed his touch. The cat watches them from the corner of the room. It looks unhappy. "You OK?" Abbott says. When his wife does not answer, he says, "Maybe we should have waited another year." Without seeming to move, Abbott's wife sheds his hands from her shoulders. He takes a step backward. With her teeth she says, "Be that as it may."

15 Abbott and the Case of the Mysterious Thing in the Driveway

"Those couches," Abbott says. "I know," his wife says. "I saw one with hexagonal arms," he says. "Did you see the one with rhinestones?" she says. "I saw that one," he says. "It also had about twenty overlapping cushions." Abbott's wife turns off the engine and opens the door. She moves both legs to the side, so that her feet are on the driveway. Then she grabs the edge of the door with her left hand and the top of the steering wheel with her right. After a deep breath, she hoists herself out of the car. Abbott gets out, too. He knows it's boring to talk about the heat, but my God it's hot. In August it is hard to believe this is Ethan Frome's hometown. As Abbott unbuckles his daughter from her seat, he sees his wife looking intently at the ground. "What is it?" he says, his head still in the car. His wife either does not hear him or ignores him. There is a big difference. He sees her kick at something in the driveway. She seems to be trying to nudge it into the grass, but without success. Then she leans down into a squat, picks the thing up, examines it, and tosses it underhanded into the grass. The motion of her toss might best be described as a *scattering,* as of birdseed or ashes. The tips of her fingers are together, her knuckles are facing up. "What was that?" Abbott says loudly. "Nothing," she says. Abbott knows it was either nothing or something. "Well, what was it?" he says. Abbott's wife comes out of her squat—the expression on her face suggests it is one of the most difficult things she has ever done with her body. Then she walks into the house without saying anything. Anyone with even the slightest knowledge of Abbott knows that he is not going to let this go. All afternoon his wife continues to say the thing in the driveway was nothing, convincing Abbott it was something indeed. He stops just short of pleading. He attempts to make his interest seem primarily academic, scientific. Then at dinner Abbott's wife casually elaborates— she says she thought the thing in the driveway was a coin but then she looked at it and found that it was not a coin. "A coin?" Abbott says. "Yes," she says. They pass food and say *please* and *thank you.* "Then what was it?" he says, trying to match her composure. "Just a little piece of foil or metal," she says. "Hm," he says. Then they tell some funny stories to the girl and have a nice family dinner. But later in bed, after the books are on the nightstands and the lights are out, Abbott says, "Let me tell you why that is a lie." Abbott's wife says, "What are you talking about?" "First," he says, "if that's all it was, some coinlike object, you would have told me right away. There would have been no reason to be so secretive. Second, if it was a coin—if you thought it was a coin—you would have tried to pick it up *before* you tried to kick it in the grass. But you tried to kick it first. Why would you kick what you thought to be a coin into the grass? You kicked first and *then* squatted down to look at it, which is not consistent with the actions of someone who thought she saw a coin and then discovered it wasn't. Come to think of it, I don't know why you would kick *a little piece of foil or metal* into the grass, either. You're someone who is concerned about the environment and also about our lawn. Not to mention the fact that when I went out there after dinner to look for it, I didn't see anything resembling the object you describe." "The object I describe," Abbott's wife says. "And speaking of squatting," Abbott says, "exactly what type of U.S. coin would entice you, in August, in the ninth month of pregnancy, to bend down and pick it up? A fifty-cent piece? A Susan B. Anthony silver dollar?" "It was a gold doubloon," she says. "Lastly," Abbott says, "nobody says *coin*. No native speaker of English would ever say, *I think I see a coin in the driveway.* You would say *quarter* or *nickel* or whatever it was, though again, I can't imagine you would bend down to pick up a nickel, knowing you may never get back up." "OK," she says. "And also, lastly, the way you threw it, your throwing motion. That was not—" "OK," Abbott's wife says. "Please stop. Do you really want to know what it was?" "Yes, I do," Abbott says, suddenly not at all sure that he does. "Fine," she says. "It was a lock of hair. I tried to kick it off the driveway, but I couldn't, so I picked it up and tossed it in the grass, using the motion you so scrupulously observed. It isn't easy to throw hair." "Hair?" he says. Abbott is momentarily confused by the fact that a lock of hair bears no resemblance to a coin, but he recovers. "A lock of hair," she says. "Probably from earlier in the summer. Maybe it blew out of the pachysandra. On the driveway it looked, I guess, *mildly* disturbing, and I knew if you saw it you would have a—" Abbott says, "What would I have?" Abbott's wife says, "You would have a reaction." So many words in the dark. Abbott has imagined all this marital talk discoloring the walls and ceiling like nicotine. "So," Abbott says, "you hid it from me, and then you lied about it all day." "That's right," his wife says. "Because I know you." The static of the monitor sounds to Abbott like the sound of his own thinking. He does not know whether his wife's deception is an instance of compassion or cruelty. Furthermore, he does not know the scale or the degree of the compassion or cruelty. It could be insignificant, but it could also represent something large, some kind of turning point. It could be the moment he understands something—either the fact that the marriage is so deep he will never touch bottom or the fact that the marriage might not work out. This would be the time to go down to the basement and walk around for a while, but his wife rolls over and puts her hand on his chest. Her hand is warm and small. The pressure of her touch is not heavy, but neither is it light.

16 Abbott and the Online Questionnaire

Abbott struggles with number seven. Reading doesn't count, and it hasn't for many years. Mowing? Dropping rocks in a grate? One thing Abbott does often in his spare time is calculate the age he will be when his children graduate from high school, from college. The age he will be when they have children, if they have children at the age he had children. There are small discrepancies in the online life-expectancy figures, but Abbott is able to conjecture that he will become a grandfather shortly after his death. Give or take a few months. But browsing actuarial tables is not a *hobby*, or at least not a healthy one like gardening.

17 In Which Abbott and His Wife Are Unafraid

Just a normal afternoon until it isn't. Until they're lying naked on the bed, testing a hypothesis. This is the thirty-seventh week. They're the first people in the history of pregnancy to try this, they're certain. And now Abbott's wife's belly is like Cape Horn—it's treacherous, but it's the only available shipping route. Abbott and his wife circumnavigate; they go the long way around, and several times their hopes are nearly dashed upon the hard, venous outcropping. They persevere, sweaty and storm-tossed. They are lucky to be alive. Something occurs, approximate to intercourse. The bottom sheet rends and pulls up, exposing the mattress. Ejaculate shimmers on Abbott's digital wristwatch. The laughter, they fear, will wake the napping girl.

18 Abbott and the Irregular Past Tense

Abbott, his wife, and his daughter are having a nice time in the family room with a big green ball. They are sitting in a triangular formation, rolling the ball back and forth to one another. The girl is doing well, though Abbott is not even thinking about her motor development in relation to average children. He's just playing ball with his family, formulating a cocktail. "Mom throwed the ball!" the girl says. "And Dad catched it!" "Hey, that's right," Abbott's wife says, raising her eyebrows at Abbott. Abbott interprets his wife's glance to mean she is impressed with the girl's verbal ability. Abbott has never told his wife this—he's never told anyone—but he has a vision of himself as a father who, in the most gentle and loving and supportive way, corrects his children's grammar. At the dinner table, say, buttering a roll and explaining, affably, the uses of *lie* and *lay*, for instance, or *which* and *that*. His intention is certainly not to demean or humiliate, and neither is it simply to instruct, really, but to share his passion and respect for the amazing system of English, its intricate rules and odd exceptions. In his mind, the strictures of grammar and syntax become a kind of fun family activity, with everyone very lovingly and entertainingly pointing out everyone else's errors. And they're all laughing and passing the corn and making up funny examples of dangling modifiers. And in this way the children are thoughtful practitioners of our language, and their sense of language, and hence thought, is (lovingly) honed. And it's not actually the children's childhood that Abbott is imagining. He's imagining the children as adults so honed and remarkable that people want to interview them, and in these interviews they speak fondly (and correctly) of the family dinner table of their youth, the father who presided warmly over speech and usage. It sounds authoritarian, they know, but it wasn't like that. It was fun. The father didn't belittle them; rather, he found a way to bring the family together around clauses and phrases, subordination and antecedent. You just have to take our word for it. His tone was remarkable. The game continues, the green ball rolling across the carpet, Abbott's wife and his daughter laughing and exclaiming. "You throwed it!" his daughter says, referring to herself. "That's right," his wife says. Abbott knows how difficult it will be to pull this off. If he misses his mark—even slightly—he's a tyrant. "And Dad catched it," his wife says. She reaches over and pats Abbott on the knee. "Right, Dad?" she says. Abbott throws the ball into the air and grabs it hard with two hands. He sticks out his tongue and makes his eyes wide. He rubs the ball on top of his head, making strands of his hair stick up. "That's right," he says, "I did."

19 In Which Abbott Stays Clean

The corn on the cob is locally grown, and it is delicious. The dinner
begins with five cooked ears on the table. Abbott and his wife eat two
ears each, leaving one for their daughter. Abbott's daughter can't eat from
the cob, or won't, or Abbott won't let her, so Abbott cuts the kernels off
with a paring knife. This will not, though, be a story about wounds of the
flesh. Abbott positions the ear vertically on his plate, much like a holder
sets a football for a field-goal attempt. He presses the top of the ear with
one hand and slices down the cob with the other. The girl does not like to
eat the corn as a spoonful of kernels. She prefers large *plaques* of corn that
she can pick up and eat with her fingers, so Abbott has to slice deeply and
forcefully into the cob. The corn and the plate are slippery with reduced-
fat butter, and the ear shoots off the plate, directly toward Abbott. With
startling celerity, Abbott pushes straight back from the table, rising to
his feet in a crouched position, arms up, legs bowed slightly to avoid the
free-falling corn. He looks, at the end of this maneuver, something like a
gymnast who has just nailed a dismount. A gymnast with a paring knife.
His chair capsizes loudly behind him as the corn passes between his legs

to the floor, where the dog, its fear trumped by appetite, begins to lick it. One instant there is Abbott's lap, the next it is gone. This is certainly Abbott's most athletic deed in years, and his initial response, as he stands from his crouch, is pride. He sure evaded that corn. He still has it, the quickness, the reflexes. But then he hears the dog gnawing the cob, and he sees his daughter's empty tray of food. He feels the upturned, surprised gazes of his wife and daughter. He notices, too, that the clothes he sought so athletically to protect are old, faded, and lightly stained. And Abbott knows—right now, not later—that his very pregnant wife, were she to be the only thing standing between the darting corn and the dog-patrolled floor, would leap or dive like a soccer goalie to preserve her offspring's dinner. Abbott rights his chair. With his foot he nudges the dog and the corn out of the way and sits down again. He has the right to remain silent, but he waives it. He speaks down to his plate. "I didn't even *think*," he says, either confessing or absolving, but in any case telling the truth.

20 Abbott Improves

Tonight Abbott cannot find his paint-can-opening tool, so he uses a flathead screwdriver instead. With a dusty garden stake he stirs the paint, even though he had it mechanically stirred earlier in the day. He places the gallon can on a folded sheet of plastic to protect the floor. All of the office and nursery furniture is out in the hallway. He removes the cardboard sleeve from the bristled end of a new two-inch cutting brush with an angled tip and wooden handle. He splurged because he's tired of bad brushes. He dips the brush, rubs one side against the lip of the can, and begins to cut above the floorboard. The paint looks light, but he knows it will darken as it dries. He moves slowly along the walls, cutting around the trim of the floor, the ceiling, the two windows and two doors. (Then around the light-switch cover, the outlet covers, and the overhead light.) The brush is excellent. He uses a damp paper towel to scrub his mistakes from the glossy trim. The cutting takes an hour and a half. Abbott keeps thinking he'll get up for a beer, but he never does. The steady deep breathing from the monitor, turned low. Abbott's movements sound strange because the room is empty. He is reminded of other empty rooms, other painted walls. He wouldn't go back if he could. How many men tonight are painting nurseries, feeling unique? When he's finished cutting, he wraps the brush tightly in a plastic bag. He pours paint from the gallon can into a sturdy plastic tray, then blots the drips from the side of the can with a paper towel. He takes the plastic covering off a yellow roller cover and pushes the cover firmly onto the roller. He slides the roller back and forth in the tray, coating the yellow cover in paint and evening out the coverage. Then he rolls a vertical strip beside the door, overlapping his brushed line. The previous paint job is a bit rough and uneven, and Abbott knows that if he really wanted to do this right, he would spend a night sanding the walls smooth. And he might prime the walls before painting. He rolls three more strips, ceiling to floor, reaching the corner. The humidity makes the paint runny and slow-drying, so he keeps this first coat light, and he watches for drips. He puts his face close to the wall and turns his head to find the right angle in the light. Abbott's wife makes her way past the furniture in the hallway and walks into the room. "This looks great," she says. He nods, inspects. "It will dry a little darker," he says. "I'm glad we didn't choose the other one," his wife says. "Me too," he says. "You think maybe just one coat?" she says. "No," Abbott says. "It'll need two." His wife says, "Can you bring in that chair for me?" Abbott walks out to the hallway and returns with his heavy wooden desk chair. He puts the chair in the center of the room, and his wife sits while he finishes the first coat.

21 Abbott Visits the Coffee Shop

While the earliest shoes that we have found are nine thousand years old, some scientists believe that humans began making rudimentary shoes as early as thirty to forty thousand years ago. Bombs date back at least as early as 1281 AD, when the Mongols lobbed powder-packed ceramic balls at the Japanese. (The shards are extant.) Two nouns, separated for centuries, finally conjoined. Two concepts made one. Do not talk to strangers, Abbott will one day warn his children. Nor to people with shoes. He sits in the coffee shop with his daughter in his lap. Her eyes are still swollen from crying. He scans the crowded room and does not see any bombs. Because he's modern, he knows this means one of two things: Either there are no bombs in the coffee shop, or there are bombs in the coffee shop.

22 Abbott's Supporting Role

This afternoon Abbott's wife shuffles into the living room and an-
nounces that their daughter's bed is covered in mold. "Right through
the pillowcase," she says, "through the pillow, onto the sheet, through
the sheet, onto the mattress pad." Abbott gets to be the calm one today.
He thinks for a moment. "I bet it's because we put her to bed with wet
hair after her bath," he says scientifically. His wife seems uninterested
in causation. "Smell this!" she says, thrusting a pink pillowcase into
Abbott's face. He smells dutifully. The odor is quite bad, but he believes
they'll all get through this. He believes they'll be stronger for it. "Moldy
bed!" she exclaims. His wife's hysteria creates in him a powerful sense
of tranquility that borders on drowsiness. This means the marriage is
working. "Is it mold or mildew?" he asks, yawning and slumping deeper
into his soft chair. He means to diagnose, not jest. "Social services won't
care!" his wife says. "I bet it happens a lot," Abbott says, "but it's one of
those things that people don't want to talk about." His wife appears to
consider this remark. "My God," she says, "we are horrible parents." "No,
we're not," Abbott mutters. "We're average parents." His wife flees the

living room with the offending linens, and her wild exit plunges Abbott into a deep, narcotic sleep. Hours later, he will learn on the Internet that mold and mildew are essentially the same thing, and also that they are much different.

23 On Dormancy

The original *Curious George* (New York: Houghton Mifflin, 1941) is making Abbott uncomfortable as he reads it to his daughter for the first time (morning, family room, carpet, sun, heat, coffee, triceratops). Perhaps it should be on a higher shelf at the library. Or perhaps it should have a warning sticker. Not *banned*, of course, Abbott would never say that. But the book is a surprise. Prior to this morning, Abbott and his daughter have read only George's entertainingly dramatic and noncontroversial adventures: *Curious George Makes Pancakes; Curious George and the Dump Truck; Curious George in the Snow; Curious George's Dream.* Now this, though, the original, in which the man with the yellow hat comes to the jungle and exploits George's preternatural curiosity to capture him in a bag and forcibly remove him from his home. And later, in the big city, George has occasion to smoke a pipe—a *pipe*—and then he gets thrown into prison. Not jail—prison. There are *rats* eating George's food. The pages of the old book are ripped and faded. Abbott's daughter loves the story. George escapes prison but then ends up at the zoo. Abbott tries to read quickly and quietly; he mumbles, points to squirrels out the window.

But the girl's attention is fixed on George's trauma. Abbott's wife calls on the cell phone from the Big Y as Abbott hoped she would. These days, they have their best talks on the phone. "I'm sorry about last night," she says. Abbott says he is too. He says, "Don't stand on that chair, honey." Abbott's wife says she had a strange dream when she finally fell asleep last night and she was going to tell Abbott about it this morning but she forgot and now she can't remember the dream. "Maybe you'll remember it," he says. "Do you need anything from the store?" she says. "I don't think so," he says. Abbott's daughter wants to read the original *Curious George* again. "I ran into a woman from yoga," Abbott's wife says, "and she was telling me about this family fair coming up, and I said thanks, we'd definitely consider it, but then afterward I realized it was on the day we're having the baby." "Yeah, so," Abbott says. "So," she says, laughing. Abbott's wife asks Abbott what they're doing, and he says they're reading the original *Curious George*. He tells her about the pipe. "This is just a hard time," Abbott's wife says. "Just a minute, honey," Abbott says, "I'm talking to Mom." Abbott's wife says, "One of these days. You know?" Abbott says, "I know. I know." He does not know what his wife means. He thinks she could mean any number of things, and he thinks he agrees with all of them.

24 Abbott Stumbles toward a Theory of Use

When the generous children's librarian gives Abbott's daughter a package of animal stickers, the girl wants to open them immediately, right there in the library. Abbott knows that if he opens the stickers, she will use them up within minutes. He kindly tells her no, explaining that she should save her stickers for a special time. Abbott's daughter ignores his answer. "Dad open these?" she says. Abbott again says no. He says, "Let's just wait and open these later, OK?" "Dad open these?" she says again. "Not now," Abbott says. "You just got them, honey," he says, which is of course his daughter's point. Why is he taking a stand on this matter? What golden application does he envision for these stickers? "Dad open these?" the girl says. "I said no," Abbott says. There is no end in sight. The child's universe has contracted to this package of animal stickers, and there is no way Abbott is going to back down now, even if he wants to, his idea being that an unreasonable position held unwaveringly amounts to good parenting. His resoluteness is a value unto itself, regardless of the foolish notion about which he is being resolute. "I want these," she says. "I know you do," Abbott says, trying to communicate his empathy. "Dad open these?" "I said no and meant it," he says. Fortunately for everyone, Abbott's wife is in the library too. "You two," she says. She opens the package with her teeth and gives the animal stickers to their daughter. Abbott knows that parents should not undermine each other's authority, but he is grateful for the intervention. The girl sits on a bench and begins to put the stickers on her neck and throat. She peels off one after another and presses them onto her skin. Shouldn't she at least save some of them? Abbott thinks. "Shouldn't she at least save some of them?" he says, but nobody answers. When the girl's neck and throat are covered, she begins putting stickers on her chin and cheeks. She uses every single animal sticker, probably two dozen. She is delighted. She smiles as she touches her face lightly with the tips of her fingers. She drops the sticker backing onto the floor, and Abbott picks it up. Abbott's wife finds a small mirror in the library dollhouse and holds it up so their daughter can see. The girl loves the stickers. The generous children's librarian who gave the stickers to Abbott's daughter walks past, waving and smiling, apparently untroubled by the prodigality. Abbott grudgingly understands that this is what the stickers were for. The stickers were for his daughter's neck and face. And he understands that had she done something different with the stickers, then that different thing would have been what the stickers were for. It is not difficult for Abbott to imagine his daughter bringing home a gentleman friend twenty-five years hence. (Make it a female lover if you want—it does not matter to the story.) Abbott, by then no doubt a full professor or perhaps even an endowed chair, will have four cocktails, and he will win over his daughter's beloved with timely allusions to Oscar Wilde and Joe Montana. Later, in bed—Abbott and his wife will allow them to sleep together—the gentleman (or whoever) will lounge dissolutely on his elbow and say, "Your parents are great. Especially your dad. He's really great." Abbott's daughter will make that face that can be traced back to infancy. She'll say, "He's mellowed a lot. When I was a kid, he was the kind of dad who wouldn't let me put stickers on my face. And he'd correct my grammar in a way that he thought was fun and loving. And he'd tell me to be careful all the time. God, he'd tell me to be careful when I was making toast." And then they will lie together in that old bed, most likely naked, and for a long time talk about fathers, the failures of fathers.

25 Abbott and the Parable of the Giraffe

Abbott's daughter is having a hard time of it indeed. She is trying to lift
the stuffed giraffe from the floor, and she cannot do it. She has been at it
for some time—nearly a minute, perhaps—and she cannot lift the giraffe.
The toy is not large, nor is it heavy. Abbott watches, refusing, out of some
combination of principle and indolence, to facilitate. He admires her
focus, her tenacity, her intrinsic dignity. She is a straight arrow of intent.
Her faint eyebrows are squeezed in concentration and purpose, but
she has not become frustrated or angry. She is leaning over, using both
hands, pulling the giraffe's head, and the world is simply not working as it
supposed to, as it has up to this point. The reason that Abbott's daughter
can't lift the giraffe is that she is standing on it. Once she steps off of the
animal, she has a much easier time lifting it, which she does, with neither
pride nor humiliation. And then, giraffe clamped in her armpit, she
moves forth to the next thing.

26 On Containment

As Aristotle probably asked, *Is it not prudent to diagnose the diagnoser?*
Briefly, then: Abbott's parents were divorced when he was nine years
old. Afterward, his parents had joint custody, so Abbott moved between
their residences every two weeks. These transfers occurred on Sundays,
in late afternoon or early evening. And there was, as in some convoluted
geocentric model of the heavens, motion within motion: His mother, with
whom Abbott lived half the time, moved six times in the eight years of the
custodial arrangement. One consequence of this Ptolemaic childhood was
that Abbott at a young age became preoccupied with luggage. Suitcases,
duffels, bags, satchels, backpacks. And not just luggage, but any item
within which other smaller items might be tidily placed. Chests, trunks,
bins, tubs, baskets, folders, cartons, envelopes, pillowcases, pockets. The
sturdy cardboard box. And tonight Abbott is in his garage, searching for
something that he forgets immediately when he sees, tucked in the corner
like some neglected pet, his rooftop carrier. It's covered in cobwebs, but
still modern and sleek. At thirteen cubic feet, it's capacious enough to
hold several large suitcases and a pair of nice water skis. (Abbott does

not water-ski.) The carrier is durable and lightweight, surprisingly easy to install upon the car's roof rack. Its latches, one on each side, can be locked and unlocked, locked and unlocked, with a small silver key that glints on Abbott's key ring. He looks for the key there, on his key ring, and eventually finds it. He holds it between his thumb and forefinger. There is an extra key he can keep in a special place. Abbott would like to take a trip. He would like, actually, to have taken a trip. He would like to return from a trip. He would like to ease the carrier manfully off the car's roof and wipe it down like a weary steed. He would like to take a firm but tender grip of its black aerodynamic flanks and then position it carefully on a custom-built pallet in the corner of the garage, which is, after all, yet another pleasing container. Abbott turns in a slow circle. He has no idea what he is in here to find. There are so many things in the garage— scattered tools, furniture, a grass-seed spreader—far more than could ever fit in the carrier. It's a discouraging mess. The space is not used well. The pallet he could probably build if he ever had time. Today is, what, Sunday? On Friday Abbott will have another child.

27 Abbott and the Small Black Spot

Abbott's daughter sits on the floor across the room from Abbott. The small black spot he sees on the side of her neck belongs to one of two categories—deer tick or not deer tick. This family room is ninety miles from Lyme, Connecticut. "Come here for a second," he says to her. "I want to check something." The girl keeps working on her fire-station puzzle. She does not come to him. Abbott is certain that the black spot is a deer tick. As he crosses the room, though, he reasons that most black spots are not deer ticks. It's fear, he knows, that turns spots into ticks. He expands his categories—mole, mud, magic marker. The black spot is very likely not a deer tick, he realizes. He crouches to his daughter's neck, and so what if the spot is a tick? So what? Some deer ticks do not carry disease, and some do not carry implication. Abbott removes the tick from her skin in the proper manner. He's not even sure it's a deer tick. He can look that up later. At present, his daughter needs help with her puzzle. The Dalmatian is tricky.

28 Abbott Looks out the Window

Long after the volunteer community search party disbanded, the missing girls have been found at a rest area four states away. They're alive. They were playing shoeless in the picnic area when an alert motorist called authorities. They're skinny, but they have always been skinny. The sheriff's deputy back home wept at the press conference. He said, "Most of us working on this one have kids. The ones with kids are the hardest." He said, "You just can't—" but he didn't finish. Abbott leans back in his chair and tries to recall which missing girls these are. The summer is full of them. Out his window he can see a maple tree, the top of a weathered wooden fence, his neighbor's roof and chimney. The window is divided into twelve panes, four rows of three. Abbott imagines that each pane is a framed photograph. He studies the composition of each of the twelve panes. He moves along rows, left to right, beginning with the upper left pane. A cloud of leaves and a single red brick. A squirrel on new shingles. Sky with faded contrail. There is not one pane that is not beautiful.

29 Abbott and the Cold Shudder

Abbott's office is nearly a nursery. The chair and books he has already moved to the basement. Only the desk remains, crowded on one side by a changing table and crib, now assembled, and on the other side by a rocking chair and a chest of drawers filled with tidy stacks of clothing that seem too small to fit anyone. Alphabet letter-cards span the walls, spaced uniformly. A Kite likes wind. A Lamb is soft. The Moon is full. Abbott stands in front of his desk, awaits connection. The room still has the new-paint smell. Today is the anniversary of tragedy, but which day is not? Abbott's eyesight is not what it used to be, but if he squints and leans down toward the laptop screen he can read, in the archival photographs, the messages handwritten on the signs held aloft by dark-skinned people trapped on rooftops of flooded buildings. One sign says HELP US, one says WE NEED WATER, one says PLEASE HELP. Darwin was troubled by the eye, its "inimitable contrivances." How could natural selection, working so gradually upon only the modest, incremental variations produced by random mutation, have created something as complex as an eye? What adaptive benefit is one one-thousandth of an optical organ? Or even half of one? "The eye to this day gives me a cold shudder," he wrote after the publication of *On the Origin of Species*. But the mechanism of the eye is the easy part to believe, as any insurance executive can tell you. "One might have thought of sight," wrote the vice president of Hartford Accident and Indemnity Company, "but who could think / Of what it sees . . . ?" Abbott's wife knocks on the open door. Abbott turns, keeps his body in front of the screen so his wife cannot see. "When are you going to move the desk?" she says. "Right this very instant," he says. Abbott DISCONNECTS NOW and crawls beneath the desk with a screwdriver. He begins to take the desk apart, keeping the screws in a sandwich bag he will affix to the inside of a drawer with masking tape. On the tape he will write DESK SCREWS in black marker. At some point during the disassembly, a juncture of interest to philosophers, the desk ceases to be a desk, the office an office.

30 Abbott on the Roof

The stars are far behind the clouds tonight as Abbott climbs a borrowed ladder to his roof. He does not have wine or a blanket. He sits on the flat roof above his family room and rests his back against the gentle slope of the garage. He presses his palms against the shingles, still warm from the day. He knows the warmth is from the late-summer sun, but it is easy to believe that it comes from inside the house, from all the bodies and breath and motion. The heat of a family, radiating out. He does not have marijuana or an old acoustic guitar. In two minutes he's self-conscious. In five minutes he's bored. In eight minutes his lower back hurts. He sees a firefly blink below him, and he counts the seconds until it blinks again. He hears his neighbors through their screens: the bright clatter of silverware on plates, spouses and children calling for one another through the houses. *Where are you? Can you come here for a second? Have you seen Matt?* Someone is running a power saw. Someone is dragging a can to the curb, though it is not, Abbott thinks, trash night. The wind pushes small sticks and branches across the roof and off the edge. No moon, no constellations, no meteor showers. Abbott climbs back down the ladder.

In the family room his wife says, "What were you doing?" Abbott fixes a drink in the kitchen. "Just checking," he says. His wife says, "Come in here." She is lying on the bad couch. The family room is still a mess from the day. "Let's clean this up later," she says. Abbott lifts her legs and sits beneath them. The veins in her ankles look terrible. You poor thing, the nurses always say. "Are you scared?" Abbott says. "Sure," she says. "Do you wish we had done the amnio?" he says. "No," she says, "I don't think about that." Abbott sees a bulging garbage bag slumped against the front door. It probably is trash night, then. "Everything is going to be fine," he says. "Look at this," she says. "Is that an elbow?" he says. "Either an elbow or a knee." Abbott tries to kiss it but it's gone. He keeps his lips on his wife's stomach for a while, then he says, "Just a second." He slips out from beneath his wife's legs and gets off the couch. He leaves the family room and walks the length of the house to the bedroom. From the drawer of his nightstand he takes a wrapped gift and returns to the family room. "This is just something small," he says. "I got you something too," his wife says. "Go get it. It's in my nightstand." Abbott walks back to the bedroom and pulls a small wrapped gift from his wife's nightstand. Then he walks back to the family room. "Did you wrap this?" his wife says, holding up the gift. Abbott shakes his head. "It's nothing big," he says. Abbott's wife begins to unwrap the gift. "You know," she says, "when I first heard you up there, I was angry. But then I realized you are not the kind of man who would ever fall off a roof."

31 Abbott Chooses a Side

Monitored, amplified, the fetal heartbeat sounds to Abbott like the hoarse
bark of a guard dog. "Or like a marching band far away," his wife says. The
nurses take her blood pressure and talk about their distant pregnancies.
"Back then they just knocked you out," says one. Then they roll Abbott's
wife out of the room. She smiles weakly and waves as she disappears.
Abbott puts on his scrubs and waits. He knows that eleven thousand
babies are born in the United States every day. Nothing else so ordinary
is ever called miraculous. He sits, stands, walks to the window. Three
stories down, morning commuters drink coffee and talk on their phones.
They do not even glance up at the Childbirth Center, this hub of life.
They do not seem to notice or care. Abbott surmises that he has driven
past dozens of births while opening CD cases or eating crackers. He sits,
stands, picks up items and puts them down. Finally someone comes for
him, leads him out. His wife is at the center of the operating room with
a drape over her chest. Abbott can choose which side of the drape: belly
or head. He chooses head, because it is crying and because he does not
want to see—ever—his wife's abdominal wall. Her headache is caused by

a rapid drop in blood pressure, and the anesthesiologist is making things better. His voice is soothing and kind through his mask. "Is it still bad?" he says. Abbott's wife nods. "In just a second you're going to start feeling better," he says. There are many people in the room. The nurses and doctors joke about speeding tickets, and Abbott wishes they would be quiet. Then they all grow quiet, and Abbott wishes they would start joking again. He does not know whether the procedure has begun. He is with his wife, though it is true that the doctors on the other side of the drape are with his wife, too. He strokes her hair through the thin fabric of her scrub cap, worried that it might not be the right thing. (Later she will tell him it was the right thing.) Her arms are out to her sides. The doctors use what sounds like a vacuum. Abbott, sitting by his wife's head, can see, over the drape, the eyes of the doctors above their masks. The birth feels secretive, covert. He can feel the hot air pooling in his own mask. The thing he'd like to tell all of them is *Please be careful with this woman and this baby*. It's always possible to be a little bit more careful. He leans down to whisper to his wife. He puts his covered lips lightly on her ear and says nothing. He makes a whispering noise but not words. The doctors tug hard at the hole they have made, and here now there's a human baby aloft over the drape, looking not at all ready for existence. Her skinny legs, for instance, are curved like parentheses. It has already happened and it is over and it has begun. The doctors begin to repair Abbott's wife's body. Her head is smiling, weeping. "Is she OK?" she asks. Someone says, "She looks great." This time the camera has fresh batteries, but Abbott forgets to take a picture. Fortunately, the anesthesiologist is there to help. Here's the red-throated howl. Here are the curled toes. Here's the knit cap too big. Here's the yellow cord with bright drops of blood. Here's the pediatrician's forearm. Here's the scale. Here's the wife, so close and so far away. Here's the terror, the full and expanding heart. Here's what happened to Abbott.

Abbott's syllabus is six pages, single-spaced. It is thorough and exact, and in its very form suggests the comforting notion that the world can be known. Additionally, the detailed schedule of readings and assignments should serve to ward off catastrophe until mid-December, at least. The teetering planet cannot collapse on October 14; there is an essay due that day. The white sheets of the syllabi are still faintly warm from the copy machine, and Abbott always feels, as he distributes them, that he is giving students something nourishing, something prepared, some baked good. He imagines a professor's apron and mitts. Abbott plans to speak for just ten minutes or so about the class, but he speaks for thirty-five minutes. He plans to be stern and intimidating, but he isn't. He plans not to allow any students to add the course, but he admits four students without even asking for their hard-luck stories. He erases the blackboard and walks to his office. Colleagues in the hallway shake his hand and congratulate him, and Abbott makes jokes about sleep. In his office he stands in front of his bookshelves. Often he has the feeling, looking at his books, that they somehow represent his own achievement. He wipes the dust from his desk with a tissue and then sits down, his back to the doorway. Through his window he can see students playing Frisbee in the bright grass. Abbott knows about the empty pie tins of the Frisbie Pie Company (1871–1958), and so he has no need to research the origins of the pastime. He is free just to watch, and he does. One must of course be cautious in making any broad assertion about human nature, but it seems to Abbott that humans like throwing and catching things in the sun. He turns on the lamp that he found beside a dumpster. Occasionally a student comes by, knocks timidly on the open door. The students are nervous and sincere. Over the summer they read the books that Abbott recommended, and they loved them. They have busy semesters, jobs. Their parents don't want them to change majors again. Abbott remembers their names. They all speak in a rush, stop abruptly, and ask if Abbott had a good summer. Yes, thanks, Abbott says, very good. He walks across campus, and the day is so beautiful that he notices it. On his skin he feels sun and breeze, the counterpoise of seasons. He is not thinking much of anything. In the parking lot he walks up and down the rows, up and down, searching for his car. Eventually he finds it. He drives, engaging the clutch, depressing the brake, tapping the turn-signal wand. At a crosswalk he looks for his sunglasses and can't find them. The car takes him right to his driveway. Inside the house he changes clothes and takes his elder daughter outside to walk around the block. The girl walks twenty-five feet past the drive-way and stops at the grate. Abbott picks up a small rock, puts it in his palm, and extends his palm toward his daughter. His daughter pinches the rock between her thumb and forefinger, then holds it over the grate for a moment before dropping it in. Abbott and his daughter listen for the sound of the rock hitting water—a faint, high-pitched *bloop* that reverberates in the dark tunnel. The girl laughs when she hears it. A spry, gray-haired woman walks up. She asks about the baby. She says many years ago her children used to sit right here and drop rocks down this same grate. "What a blessing," she says, and then she walks off. Abbott and his daughter drop a few more rocks, enjoying the sound of the rocks hitting the water. Then they walk around the block. Precisely halfway, the girl asks to be picked up, so Abbott picks her up and carries her back to the house. "You're getting so big," he says over and over. The baby is asleep, and Abbott's wife tells Abbott to take a nap if he wants. Abbott sleeps for twenty minutes and wakes up disoriented. In the bathroom he does not look in the mirror. The baby is up now, and he holds her in the family room while his other daughter plays with a blue tractor and his wife makes dinner. With one hand he helps his daughter make a ramp out of a large book, and they roll the tractor down the ramp. He helps her make a wall of blocks, and they roll the tractor down the ramp and into the wall of blocks. She puts four necklaces on Abbott and tries to put one on the baby. "Let's not do that," Abbott says. Then the girl pinches her finger in the jewelry box and cries. "Ouch," Abbott says. "Let's take a look at that." At dinner, the baby lies quietly in the bassinet while mowers drone outside. "This is not a good dinner," the girl says, but she eats quite a bit. "These are the last of the great tomatoes," Abbott's wife says. After dinner, the girl jumps on her new trampoline and then takes a bath. Abbott sits on the floor of the bathroom beside the tub. The tub has a shower door that slides on a track, so he can't sit on the edge. He examines the frame of the sliding door, wondering how difficult it would be to remove. He can only imagine what has grown beneath the metal. He could remove the frame, clean the tub beneath, install a hanging rod and shower curtain. It would be a nice surprise for his wife, who hates this shower door. The girl drinks bathwater out of colored plastic cups. There are at least twenty-five plastic animals in the water, representing numerous epochs and ecological zones. All of them sink except, inexplicably, Big Zebra. Abbott is not worried, at present, about lead paint on the animals leaching into the water, in effect creating a toxic lead bath. He dries the girl off and then puts on her diaper and pajamas. Abbott's wife puts the girl to bed. The baby is happy in her bassinet, so Abbott cleans up the bathroom and then the kitchen. The dishwasher is old and ineffective, so he has to scrub the plates and glasses thoroughly in the sink before loading them. The falling sun slants through the window above the sink and illuminates the plastic oral syringes on the sill. When he's finished with the dishes, he wipes down the counters. He needs a haircut. His wife walks gingerly through the kitchen and pats Abbott on the hip. "How do you feel?" he says. "Not bad," she says. She turns on the girl's monitor and then, grimacing, lifts the baby out of the bassinet. "You should let me do that," Abbott says. He sniffs the sponge and props it against the Cold knob in the sink. Abbott's wife nurses the baby while Abbott feeds the dog and the cat, then cleans up the family room. He puts the jewelry in the box, the buttons in the coffee can, the stuffed animals in the crate. On the monitor he can hear his daughter singing an English folk song about the bubonic plague. He lies on the carpet, listening. The sun goes down and the room grows dark. Abbott gets off the floor and turns on a lamp. Then he sits on the couch next to his wife and helps her stare into the baby's face. It's a second conception—together they bring her into the world.

ACKNOWLEDGMENTS

For their material, editorial, and/or moral support, I would like to thank: my family, near and far; the persistent Lisa Bankoff; the handy Bob Bourke; the meticulous Susan Murray; the heroes at LSU Press, particularly John Easterly, Lee Sioles, and MaryKatherine Callaway; and the editors of the *Cincinnati Review, Subtropics, StorySouth,* and *Best of the Web 2010,* where versions of some chapters were originally published. I owe special mention to Michael Griffith, who made every page better. Always and especially I am grateful to Jenn Habel, the center and the reason.

CPSIA information can be obtained
at www.ICGtesting.com
Printed in the USA
LVOW03s1953080218
565817LV00002B/230/P